C00 991 452X
CANCELLED

D0226954

This is my first attempt at writing a children's story for publication. My last employment was with The Department of the Environment as a Technical Officer. This involved overseeing maintenance and installations in government military and civil establishments in the area allotted to me.
I am widowed with two girls. The eldest has two boys and the youngest two girls who were in my thoughts when writing this story.

I dedicate this book to the memory of my wife Margaret.

Hugh Galt McKenzie

THE FOUR DREAMERS OF STRATHBROCHAN

AUSTIN MACAULEY
PUBLISHERS LTD.

A CIP catalogue record for this title is available from the British Library.

ISBN 978149634618

www.austinmacauley.com

First Published (2014)
Austin Macauley Publishers Ltd.
25 Canada Square
Canary Wharf
London
E14 5LB

Printed and bound in Great Britain

Acknowledgments

Thanks to information provided by the Paisley Library and the Readers Digest reference dictionary.

Contents

Introduction

The book is written with some factual and some fictitious links to the past as imagined through the eyes of the children in the story. The children give their explanations and meanings to many of the questions that may never be answered.

Supposing events in time do live on in space, then the stories will appeal to children's imagination and as there are factual events from history involved in the episodes of each chapter, this could be an incentive for children to take an interest in historic events.

As the "Four Dreamers" wander through events of the distant and not so distant past the limits to their travels seem endless and the story is controlled. This is to halt the journeys into the past becoming a monotonous theme and making the book boring.

The village of Strathbrochan and Loch Brochan as well as the characters of the village are purely fictitious, with the possibility that someone may link the story to an area of Scotland.

The author's coloured drawings will provide a visual help for children to understand the descriptions of the strange happenings the main characters are confronted with.

Although the tales in the book are of the past, the situations in the chapters are frequently discussed, or portrayed in television documentaries, or the national press and children watching, or reading about them will immediately remember the four dreamers being there and this will arouse an interest and be educational.

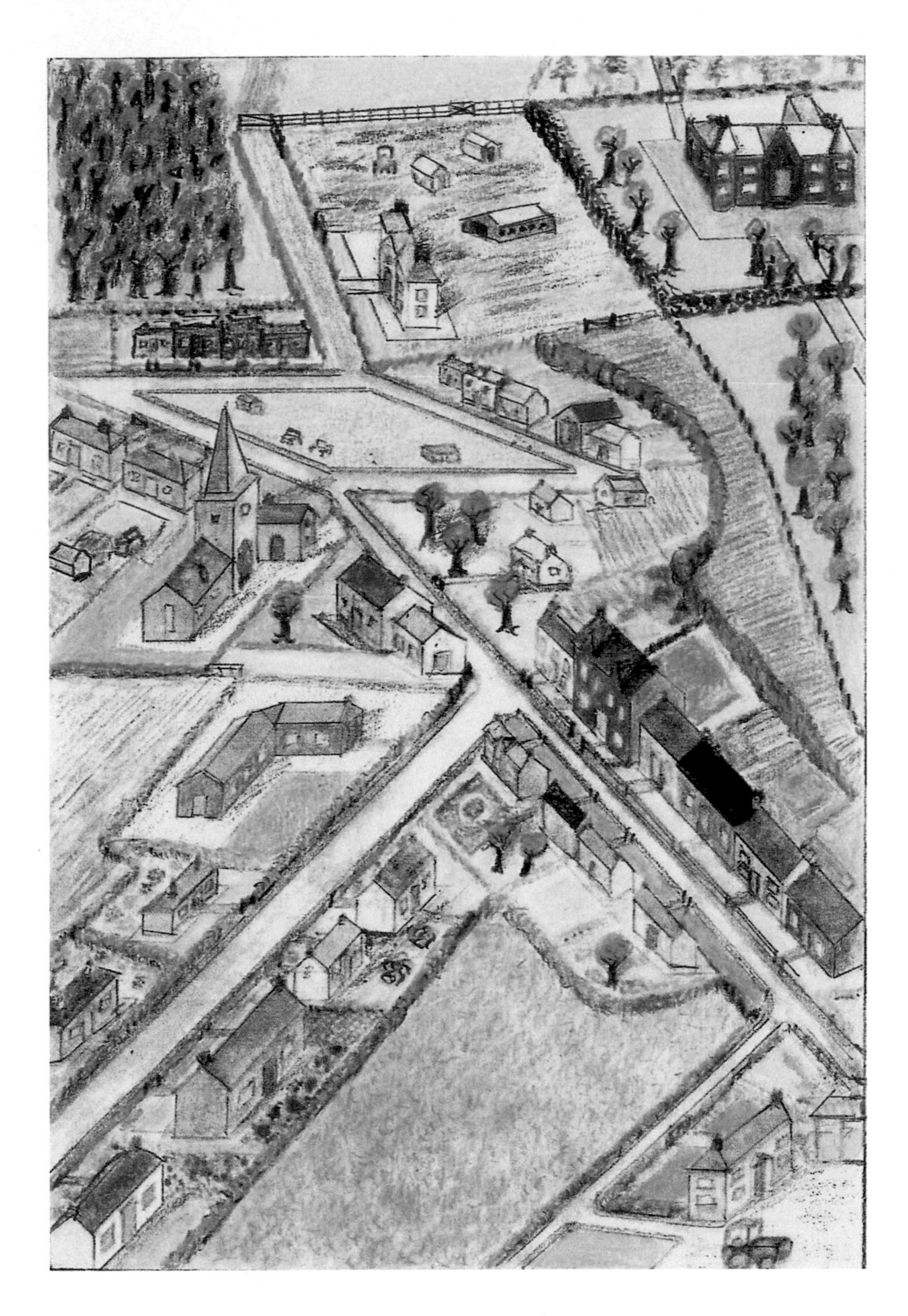

Strathbrochan from the sky

1
Strange Happenings at Loch Brochan

There is a quiet little village in the Scottish Highlands called Strathbrochan. It is a small community of around 400 people. A general store run by Angus MacGregor provides for most of the villagers needs, as the nearest towns of Aberfeldy and Pitlochry are over twenty miles away. The store is a centre of village gossip where things are spoken of in supposed confidentiality.

The local employment is mainly in the rural activities and on the local estate, which is owned by Colonel and Lady Maxwell; who take a keen interest in the village affairs. In general the village is a fine place to live and a helping hand is always available to anyone in need. The villagers are all well known to each other and life is taken as it comes at an easy pace.

A small hotel called "The Pheasant" caters for visitors to the area, and local functions. The restaurant and bar are well frequented. The hotel is run by Graham and Margaret Morrison and the hotel has been in the Morrison family for over sixty years.

The village minister, Mr Wilson, lives with his wife Gladys in the manse and he and Father O'Brian look after the other spiritual needs of the villagers in their little churches. Sunday is still a special day in Strathbrochan.

Miss MacTaggart is the local school head teacher and she educates the village children from the ages of five to twelve with part-time help from assistant teachers when available. She is very strict and stands no nonsense, but even so, you will never find a child with a cross word about their teacher. Miss MacTaggart copes remarkably well in this difficult situation and thoroughly enjoys the challenge.

Other important people in the community are Dr Nichols and district nurse Mary Simpson, who care for the health of the villagers and the surrounding farming area.

Mobile help is a great advantage with a library service twice a week on Mondays and Thursdays. Weekly visits from Andy Roberts the butcher and Eddy Caldwell the fishmonger, both operating from Pitlochry, are welcome and they consider themselves as part of the village.

The village has the usual "Worthies" found in small communities, like old Tom Mitchell who can always be found around the hotel bar telling tales to anyone who will listen and hopefully buy him a drink. There is also Archie Reid who although his family are never short of a bit of salmon, rabbit, pheasant or a venison steak, will never admit to being a poacher and he is far too clever to give the gamekeeper John Hunter, a chance to catch him. It is a battle of wits between those two and it is John Hunter's ambition to catch Archie in the act one day. If he did, it would probably result in Archie having to buy the next round at one of their frequent visits to the Pheasant Hotel bar.

The only other rivalry is between farmer Smith and farmer Baxter. They both have farms on Colonel Maxwell's estate at opposite ends of the village from each other. They will always take the chance to keep an eye on the crops and animals on the other's farm and copy any new methods being employed. This is so that they will not be out-done when it comes to market day. However, at harvest time it is a joint effort to ensure all the work is completed before winter sets in, as the winters can be very severe in this area.

Now if Tom Mitchell had a rival at story telling it would be the aptly named "Four Dreamers". Four of the village children noted for telling weird and wonderful stories of things they had dreamt about. The four had a wanderlust and they liked to go off into the countryside to explore. They all had vivid imaginations and each one could make up a story to explain any unusual thing they might find. The children's names are Calum Alexander, who is twelve, Torquil McPherson is eleven, Morag Stewart is eleven and Flora Walker is ten.

Flora had one pet hate and that was when some of her classmates tried to give her the nickname Margie.

Now one pleasant summer's evening Calum, Morag, Torquil and Flora were walking along the side of Loch Brochan looking for something to take up their attention. Calum was looking up at a lonely cloud high up in the sky when he noticed a shiny light just beyond the cloud. He thought it was strange to see a star on a sunny day and he pointed it out to his friends. Immediately weird explanations flowed from each of them. Calum thought it was a little moon lit up by the sun. Torquil said it was a lost star waiting for nightfall to join its friends. Morag said it was a light to brighten up the little cloud while Flora explained that it was the sun shining on an aeroplane. As the four watched the object it was coming closer and closer and growing bigger and bigger. It was travelling at a tremendous speed and they realised that it was coming in their direction. They became terror stricken and they were rooted to the spot in fear. In their fright they were all clutching each other's hands as they huddled together with their eyes shut. Only Torquil kept one eye open and watching the huge object hurtling down. As he watched he could see smaller pieces breaking off before everything plunged down into the middle of Loch Brochan with a tremendous splash and as the object was white-hot it threw up a great cloud of steam and water vapour and the waters of the loch seemed to boil.

The great cloud of steam rose high in the sky and then as they all watched it moved towards them and the water vapour cloud dropped down and swirled all around them until they were shrouded in the cloud. While they were in the cloud they all imagined that they were in another place and they saw strange images they could not understand.

As they stood there a great wave caused by the comet plunging into the loch hit the shore and although they were quite high above the loch, it surged up until it was covering their ankles. They turned and ran as fast as they could with their excitement boiling over. What would the villagers say when they told them what had happened?

The Thing From Outer Space

Of course when they did get back to the village in their excited state and started to tell of the great object, which Calum was now calling a comet, no-one believed them, because of their vivid imaginations and their telling of so many weird dreams. Their parents gave them a right talking to and said that they had fallen in the loch and were trying to make up an excuse for being so wet. They were warned to be careful and keep away from Loch Brochan. All through the night and the following day in class the children could think of nothing else but the experience of the previous night. After dinner that day and although warned about going back to Loch Brochan, the four dreamers headed out past Mr Smith's farm on the way to the loch. They knew that they had not fallen in the water.

It was very quiet as they stood on the very spot where they had first seen the light in the sky. Calum said, "Let's hold hands like we did yesterday and see if we can feel the presence of the strange images we saw while we were in the cloud." They all joined hands and they looked across the water. All was quiet, or was it? Flora said, "Look at the mist coming up from the centre of the loch." Indeed a column of mist was rising and it rose high in the sky before bending over towards the four and dropping down to swirl around them. Immediately the four dreamers felt as if they were in a dream and were being carried away. They could sense the strange images they had seen the last time the mist had covered them.

After what seemed a long time the mist cleared and the children stood in awe at what they saw. Gone was Loch Brochan and instead they were standing on a sandy shore with sea waves breaking the silence as they hit the beach. Across on the other side of a bay was a range of low-lying hills and there was no one in sight. No buildings were visible and they could see for a long distance around, as there were no trees to obstruct their view. "I think that we should walk along the shore and maybe find someone before it gets dark," said Morag and they set off along the beach. They had not gone very far when Torquil said, "Look there are footprints in the sand. Someone has walked along here in their bare feet."

"Let's follow them," said Flora, "I am getting frightened." The footprints were heading further away from the shore and heading towards high sand dunes.

A wind started to blow and it grew stronger as they walked. Suddenly Torquil said, "Listen." All was quiet except for the sound of the wind. "There it is again," said Torquil.

"I heard it too," said Morag, "It sounded like voices."

The sounds were coming from what seemed to be a low section of ground ahead surrounded by sand dunes. They crept closer through the sand dunes and peered through the tough grass to see a number of people, not like themselves, but still with human form and dressed in furs and animal skins. They were all chattering in unintelligible sounds, more like a succession of grunts. There were family groups with women and children all seemingly very busy.

There were cave-like spaces cut into the sand dunes creating living areas for the families with large stones holding back the sand and creating separate chambers. Large flat stones were used as tables and hollowed out stones, possibly used to hold liquids. In the centre area there was what looked like a barbecue place walled off with stones where food could be prepared and there were some animal, or whale carcasses and fish lying around.

Scara. Brae

What seemed strange was that the people were very excited and collecting things to put into bundles. Watching was becoming difficult and they were afraid to go down and try and speak to these people in case they might be savages. The wind was getting very strong and blowing sand over the children. The noise of the wind, however, prevented them from hearing the approach of some men from this tribe coming up behind them. When the men came to them a strange thing happened. The men walked right through them and did not even see them. Nor did the four dreamers feel the men walking through them as they walked on down to join the rest of the tribe.

With much waving of arms and stone weapons of some sort, the excitement increased and they finally picked up the bundles that had been prepared and every one of the tribe started to leave what was their homes and soon the four dreamers were left with only the wind howling and the crash of waves from the now stormy sea.

Calum was the first to speak, "I have been here before. I remember going to the Orkney Island on holiday with my mum and dad and we were taken to a place called Skara Brae that been buried in the sand for the last 4,000 years before being discovered by archaeologists. It is now a favourite place for people visiting Orkney to go to. Do you know what this means?"

"No," said Morag.

"Well," said Calum, "I heard that things that happen on earth have a point in time and this point goes on for ever out into space travelling at the speed of light. If we could travel fast enough we would be able to reach those points and see things that happened thousands of years ago. I believe that somehow the thing we saw crashing from the sky was a planet from many light years ago that broke free and hurtled to earth as a meteorite. This meteorite has brought all the points of history that have travelled to it from earth back to the earth and somehow we can now experience things that happened long, long ago. In fact we have just seen the prehistoric men from the Stone Age walk straight through us, we are in fact ghosts from the future returning to the past and look we are leaving no footprints in the sand."

Now the explanation given by Calum may be a bit far fetched, but it was sufficient to leave the others in deep thought. The howling wind became stronger and it was blowing the sand into the homes of the Stone Age people and as they watched the small hamlet gradually disappeared under the sand that was blown from the dunes and the four dreamers knew that it would be many thousands of years before it was ever seen again.

Flora was the first to speak, "I want to go home," she cried. "What are we going to do?"

"I don't know," said Torquil. "Maybe we will be here for ever.

Morag was deep in thought and she answered, "Remember we had to hold hands before we could feel any effect from the thing in the loch. Have you noticed that we are still clasping each other's hands and that we have never let go in the excitement of what was going to happen next."

"Yes," said Calum, "you are right, let's see what happens when we let go of each other's hands." This they did and immediately a mist surrounded them and just as suddenly it lifted and they were all back on the banks of Loch Brochan at the exact spot where the adventure had started on a lovely summer's night.

They were all amazed and wondered how long they had been away, so they hurried back to Strathbrochan and were again astounded on meeting Torquil's father, Mr MacPherson, who asked if they had a good walk.

"Yes," said Torquil. There was no point in mentioning Skara Brae.

2
Great Pillars of Rock

It was a few days before the opportunity arose for the four dreamers to return to Loch Brochan. It was raining heavily the first night and they stayed indoors. The next night Calum was visiting relations with his mum and dad, Mr and Mrs Alexander. The following night Flora had an upset tummy and her mother, Mrs Walker had to take her to the doctor.

On the first night they could all manage it was as quick as they could get dinner finished to see what awaited them at Loch Brochan and another adventure. This time, however, it was decided to try and convince three other friends of theirs and they asked them to go with them to Loch Brochan so that at least someone would believe their story. The three friends were Angus, Donald and Kirsty and although they agreed to go it was more or less just for a laugh, as they did not believe the stories of the four dreamers.

The seven children set off and they soon reached Loch Brochan. Calum explained that the magic from the thing in the loch only worked when everybody joined hands and so the children firmly clasped their hands. Angus began to really believe that something was going to happen and was a bit nervous. The seven children gazed out over the loch scanning every inch to see if anything was moving. After a few minutes Donald said, "I don't see anything at all." But Calum said "Wait a little bit longer." Quarter of an hour passed and there was not a ripple on the loch's surface. The four dreamers felt very silly and Donald and Angus burst out laughing. On the way back to Strathbrochan the group walked in silence except for an occasional outburst of giggling from Kirsty. The last thing the four dreamers wanted to do that night was to tell any stories.

Torquil could not get Loch Brochan out of his mind and he was now convinced that only Calum, Morag, Flora and himself had received some power from the water vapour that swirled around them on the day the meteorite had crashed into the loch. This enabled them to somehow have access to the events from the past brought back to earth by the meteorite. He was determined more than ever to go back to the loch and try again, but the next time it would only be the four dreamers.

At the first opportunity Calum, Morag, Flora and Torquil set out on another trip to Loch Brochan. On the same spot they stood on when they had first seen the meteorite, or comet, they were not sure what it was; the four clasped their hands tightly and watched the surface of the loch. The effect was almost immediate as the waters started to boil and the vapour rose and swung towards them engulfing them in the mist. This was not a dream.

The usual feeling of travelling through space with the strange, vivid images all around them, of things from the past. What image of the past would they end up at on this ghostly visit from the future? That was the big question.

When the mist lifted the children were standing on bleak moorland. It was dull and a slight drizzle of rain was falling. The sun was just rising and soon the rain stopped and it became a fine morning. Far to their left they could hear the sound of rocks falling and they made their way towards the sound. As they got closer to the sound they could distinctly hear voices and they moved cautiously forward to the brow of a small hill. From the hill the moor swept down to the sea and it was from here the sounds of activity were coming.

Knowing from their Skara Brae visit the children were aware of the fact they were more or less ghosts and could not be seen or heard, but they still crept forward with caution to look on to a rocky coastline. Along the north-west coast of Scotland there can be seen huge pillars of rock sticking up from the sea, where the stormy seas had sculpted them through the ages. Pillars like those were the objects of the activity below. There was a group of men clad in animal skins. They were bearded and powerful looking and Calum said, "I think we are back in the Stone Age and these men are the ancient Picts." Armed with big stone hammer-like tools the men were working feverishly breaking the rock at the base of the huge pillars. The pillars looked as if they would be surrounded by the sea when the tide came in and this seemed to be the reason for the hurry. Along the shore a number of the pillars had already been knocked down.

Collecting The Stone Columns

What on earth are they wanting those long rocks for was the question asked by Flora. There was silence from her three friends who were asking themselves the same question. The pillars of rock were about twenty feet or more in length. A tremendous crash followed by another saw two pillars end up lying on the rocky shore to the delighted roar from the wild looking men. Twenty of those pillars were now lying on the shore.

Seemingly content with the number of stone pillars on the beach, the men started walking along the shore to where a pillar had already been dragged up on to the moor. The four dreamers could not believe that those men had managed to lift the pillar off the beach, but as they watched another group of men appeared from the far end of the shore and they were bringing a small herd of animals from a little cove. Men were tying ropes that looked as if they were made from animal skins, seaweed and tough grasses all plaited together round the heavy ends of the large pillars. When the animals came closer the children had never seen anything like them. They looked like a mixture of bison, ox and their native highland cattle, but they were very big and powerful beasts. The animals looked ferocious, but at the same time they were very tame and stood quietly as the men tied the other ends of the ropes round their shoulders like a harness. The largest stone had two animals harnessed to it.

Four fearsome men approached dressed in long cloaks of animal skins and they started to walk over the moor away from the sea. Calum said, "These men must be the Druid Priests." Urging the animals to pull, the pillars started to move and the procession of animals, men and pillars followed the priests over the moorland.

Calum, Torquil, Morag and Flora walked ahead of the procession, just behind the priests for what seemed like an awful long distance until they came to an area where deep holes had been dug in special positions planned by the priests. The holes must have been six to eight feet deep and each hole had a trench leading away from it in the direction the pillars were being pulled from. The trenches were more than half the length of the pillars and sloped up to the ground level, where a large flat stone was laid across each of them. "They must be going to put those pillars into these holes," said Calum.

The children were amazed at the skill and thought that must have been put into the planning of this huge and laborious task and for what reason was a great mystery. With all the benefits of science and modern day machinery this would have been a major job for our engineers to carry out. The beliefs of those druid worshipers had given them the knowledge they required to perform such a tremendous undertaking with the primitive tools at their disposal. The childrens' admiration for these people was growing by the minute. When the procession of men, animals and pillars reached the prepared area the pillars were hauled over the stones at the start of each trench until they reached the deep hole. The animals were brought back and as they did this the end of the pillar dropped down into the hole, causing the other end to rise high in the air. The ropes were removed from the animals and pillars.

The ropes were then tied to the other end of the pillar at the highest point and the other ends again harnessed to the animals. With an almighty pull the pillar was hauled up until it was standing up straight in the deep hole. At this point the men threw large stones around the bottom of the pillar and then filled the holes and trenches. All the pillars were raised in the same way until the work was completed and it looked like a forest of pillars. Morag said, "All this work just seems a silly thing to do. What good are a lot of stones sticking up out of the ground going to do?"

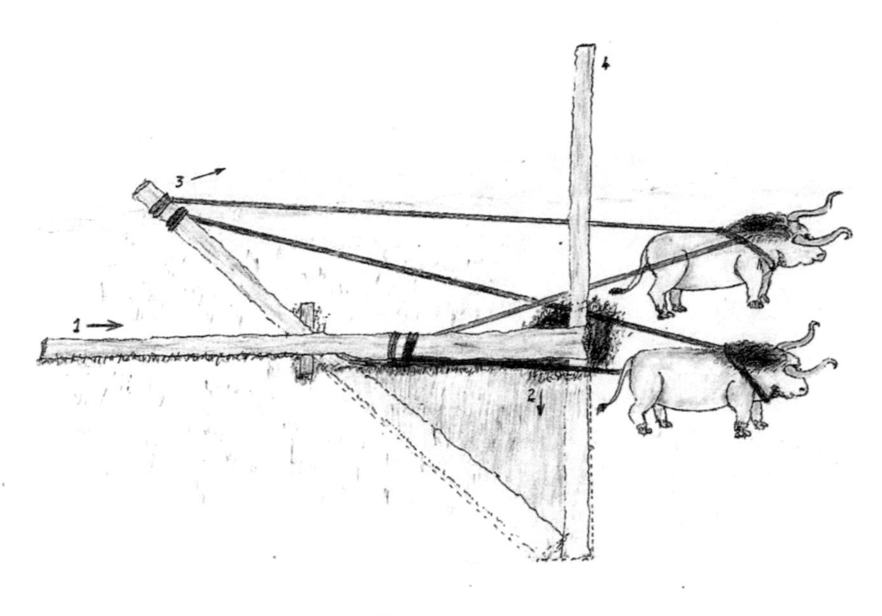

Raising The Callanish Stones

It was Torquil who noticed that there was some logic to the position the pillars had been placed in. He said, "When we came the sun was rising in that direction and a large pillar has been placed there and this represents the east. In line with this from the east another large pillar could represent sundown in the west. There are also pillars on either side of these two pillars and they could be north and south. Notice too that they have formed an avenue with smaller pillars in the direction the pillars have been brought from." He had no explanation for the thirteen other pillars around a large central pillar, but he said, "I have read about the Callanish Stones and I think that this must be them. They are on the island of Lewis near Stornoway and we have just seen them being erected."

As the whole operation had been witnessed over the day they arrived, all through the night and all the next day, it was surprising that the children had not fallen asleep, but they never felt tired and remained engrossed in the work with their hands firmly clasped as they wanted to see the work completed.

It was just as if they were dreaming and there are no better people suited to this than the four dreamers.

Trying to find a reasonable explanation Calum said, "I think there is a connection between the sun and the moon because both cast shadows from the pillars."

Torquil said," I think the upright pillars are a cathedral to worship the druid gods from all quarters of the earth."

Morag said she thought the pillars were the objects being worshipped and each one represented some heathen god of the druids. Flora said that because the pillars were brought from the sea and the path from the sea was marked out with pillars, the pillars were worshipped as gods from the sea.

The true reason for the Stone Circles of Callanish will never be known.

As the children watched the Druid Priests started to chant as they stood at the biggest stone pillar in the centre of the circle. All the Picts gathered round and one of the animals that had helped to pull the pillars into position was led to the Druid Priests. “I think they are going to make a sacrifice to their gods,” said Torquil. As one, the other three said, “We don’t want to see that.” With that statement they all unclasped their hands.

A mist surrounded them and once again when it cleared they were on the shore of Loch Brochan. They hurried back to the village thinking that people would be out searching for them, but to their surprise they were not away any longer than what was usual for them.

The next day in class it was a coincidence that Miss MacTaggart had decided to give a lesson on the ancient Brits and she used the Callanish Stones in her lecture. She told of the stone circle with a central pillar. She said, “There are twelve stones in the circle around the central pillar. At this point Calum put his hand up. “Excuse me Miss MacTaggart. There are more than twelve stones in the circle”, he said.

Miss MacTaggart thought for a moment. “Do you know I think you are right Calum. You said that as if you have visited the Callanish Stones. Have you been there?”

“Yes,” said Calum, but not as Miss MacTaggart thought and there was a smile on the faces of Flora, Morag and Torquil.

The Callanish Stones

3
Strathbrochan Highland Games

Every year Strathbrochan held their Highland Games week and this was the highlight of the year with many visitors coming to the village. During this week the wearing of the kilt and all things tartan made this a very colourful occasion.

Strongmen from far and wide competed in tossing the caber, throwing the hammer and putting the shot. Unfortunately, a visiting competitor usually won these events and it was the aim of the local strongmen to win one of those events one year. If they did they would become the local hero and probably be well remembered in the history of the village. This would also give old Tom Mitchell some new material for his tales, which no doubt would be greatly exaggerated.

The other athletic events were the sprints, 100, 200, 400 and 800 metre races. With the tougher long distance cross-country races, for which there was a tremendous interest.

Training for the Strathbrochan Highland Games

There was Highland dancing, which Morag was entering for her third year and she was hoping that third time would be lucky and win the best dancer award. A big attraction of the games was the keenly contested pipe band events and the Scottish fiddle and accordion band competition, where the winners had the prestige of playing at the Grand Ceilidh on the final night of the games.

Other events were for the best garden vegetables and flowers on display.

Cookery and different types of baking usually made it very hard for the judges to come to a decision. Their decision did not always meet with the approval of some contestants.

The children competed for prizes in the obstacle race, the egg and spoon race, the wheelbarrow and the sack race

This year the games were a complete success and beyond everyone's expectations. For the junior Highland Dancing event third time was very lucky for Morag, who won her event with the highest points ever awarded to a dancer at the games. Our other three dreamers also did very well. Flora won the 100 metres race for her age group, Calum won his 100 metre race and Torquil came in a very good second in the more difficult children's cross country race. They were all delighted with their prizes.

Archie Reid won the best garden vegetable display prize to the annoyance of John Hunter who was expected to win as he had done in previous years. Hamish Wilson's wife Gladys won the best pastry prize and Mrs Baxter, the farmer's wife, won the fancy cakes prize. Some of the judging was done by Lady Maxwell and all the prizes were presented by Colonel and Lady Maxwell, who had kept a great secret from the winners list and as they announced that Mr Alexander had won the prize for the best performance in the strongman section with the highest points won over the three events, a great roar erupted from the villagers. Here at last one of the villagers had beaten all comers as the games strongest man. The farmers were not engaged in the games events, but Mr Smith and Mr Baxter got a special mention due to them taking visitors on tractor and horse and buggy rides around the estate and for the high quality of the farm produce that was on sale to the public.

Due to the Highland Games the four dreamers were involved in helping out during the week and when the school holidays started this was the time for family holidays. Calum was going to Blackpool for a week with his parents. The following week Torquil was going to Spain for two weeks with his parents and older sister Jean.

Morag's family were not going on holiday until September, when Mrs Stewart was going to visit her mother in Belfast. Flora was going to live with an aunt in Scarborough for two weeks.

All through the holidays the four dreamers were thinking where there next visit to the past would take them, but it did not prevent them from enjoying their holidays, or from dreaming up some wonderful tales to tell of adventures on holiday. The most exciting of these was Calum's story. He told of the thrills he experienced on the Big Dipper and the other rides in the amusement park. He said that on some of the rides when they had climbed up to the top of a section and saw the steep drop down in front of them, he wished that he could get off and was terrified, but at the end of the run he admitted that he enjoyed the thrill and looked forward to the next one.

4
An Unpleasant Experience

Due to all the summer activities it was about three weeks before Calum, Morag, Torquil and Flora could all meet again at the same time and this came about one Tuesday afternoon after lunch. It seemed such a long time since they had visited Loch Brochan and they had doubts as to whether the power of the loch would still be there. On reaching the loch at their favourite spot the four dreamers clasped their hands. All their doubts vanished as the waters in the centre of the loch started to boil. The usual column of vapour arose, swept across the loch and engulfed them in mist. The previous sensations of strange objects flashed through their minds as they were propelled to their next adventure.

The mist around them cleared and they found themselves in open country with the light of day fading. The sound of many weary feet trudging towards them heralded the arrival of a completely dishevelled army of soldiers. It looked as if they had been marching all day and they had the look of an army that had just been beaten in battle. Occasionally a shout of "Down with King George" rent the air to be followed by the various battle cries of the clans forming the army. It was a really sad sight to see these proud soldiers in such a sorry state.

As the army of thousands of men marched past it was Morag who realised what they were witnessing. Part of her school history exam had been on the history of Scotland. She had read about the Jacobite army of Prince Charles Edward Stuart, (known as Bonnie Prince Charlie) and of his army having won a battle at Falkirk. Although he won this battle his troops suffered greatly and many deserted, this resulted in the sad sight they were witnessing now.

In spite of advice from many people Charles still believed that he could defeat the English army again, but this time The Duke of Cumberland had mustered a far superior army to the English army defeated at Falkirk, both in numbers and weaponry and they were marching to Culloden with fresh and well trained soldiers.

On the fateful day of 16 April 1746, both armies faced each other on Drummossie Muir. The four dreamers were terrified as they realised what they were about to see. They huddled together behind the old Leanach Cottage and the battle began. The first charge by the Duke's army split Charles' army into two, causing chaos in the ranks. It was all over very quickly and a great slaughter took place as Charles Edward Stuart's army fled from the battlefield. The children covered their eyes at the sight of the dead bodies and the screams of the dying men filled the air. Prince Charlie had fled as the first charge split his army to be hunted across Scotland before finally escaping to France, never to return. This was the end of the Jacobite rebellion.

Morag, Calum, Flora and Torquil turned away from the awful sight as Cumberland's men slew all the injured without mercy. Those who fled and were lucky to escape were few in number and this was the last battle on

Scottish soil.

The four dreamers remained huddled by the cottage in shock at what they had seen. After what must have been many hours people appeared and started to bury the bodies on the Muir, both Jacobite and English. The children watched without speaking a word until the gruesome work was finished. “I think we should go now,” said Calum and they walked across the field to pass through a forest where someone had written “The Camerons are buried here.” While walking through the forest where the graves were, not a bird chirped, not even the rustle of the wind in the trees. There was complete silence. It was obvious that this forest would be a sacred place for the clan Cameron for many years to come, Torquil said, “ We will have to realise that all our trips into the past are not going to be pleasant.

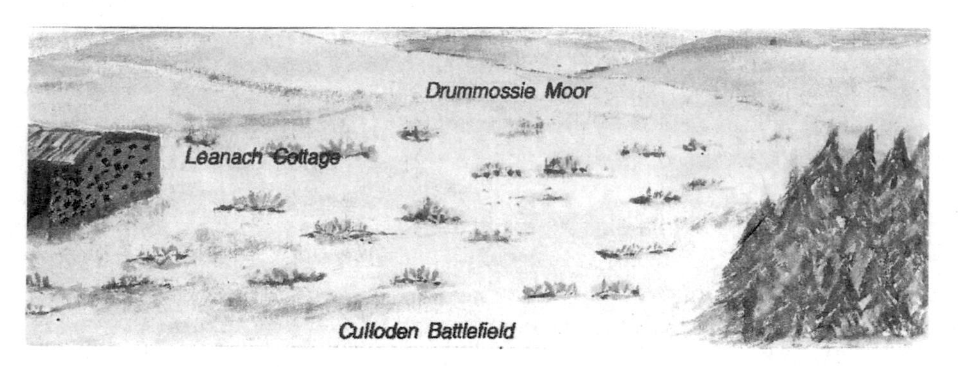

Flora said, “I want to go home.” They unclasped their hands to welcome the mist that surrounded them. They would never forget this trip into the past. It was a great relief to arrive back on the shore of Loch Brochan and get back to their families and friends in Strathbrochan.

5
A Trip Across the Ocean

It was Thursday at two o'clock when the four dreamers were able to meet again and they were wondering if it would be wise to try and make another trip to Loch Brochan after the horrific experience they had when witnessing the battle on Drummossie Muir at Culloden.

Calum said, "We have been given a special privilege to visit scenes from the past and this is a gift we should not reject. I vote that we give the power of the loch meteorite another try and just accept whatever time in history it returns us to." This little speech was all that was required to get a "yes" from the other three, although quite reluctantly from Flora, who had a nightmare after the last experience.

As it was still early afternoon they headed straight for Loch Brochan. "I wonder if the power of the meteorite is as effective at the far end of the loch," said Morag. "We will try it from there and see." They decided to do this and it was quite a long way to the other end of the loch.

Arriving at a sandy spot on the shore the four children joined hands and waited. The now familiar boiling of the water in the centre of the loch threw up the column of vapour high above the loch. It swayed for a short time as if it was looking for them before it headed towards them and they were shrouded in mist.

There was no difference in the sensation of being transported through time as there was from the usual position they started from. The strange visions flashed through their minds and they all had one thought in mind and that was that they would not witness another battle,

A tremendous blast of ships horns, sirens and hooters, anything that could make a sound was heralding the start of some great event. As the four dreamers looked around they were surrounded by hundreds of people waving to well-wishers on the dock far below. There were banners and streamers hanging from every building and lamppost.

Suddenly the air was split by the deafening roar of the ships horn and the huge mooring ropes were released from the dock. The ship slowly moved from the dock under the power of some small tugboats. As the ship moved from the dock Torquil noticed the name of Southampton on the harbour wall and as he looked up to the decks he saw lifeboats lined end to end above and his eye rested on the name on a lifeboat. He let out a loud roar. “We are on the *Queen Mary* and are going to America. We must be on the maiden voyage of the *Queen Mary* the greatest liner the world has ever seen.” He could hardly control his excitement. The worry of being on another frightening trip into the past disappeared and this would be a wonderful experience.

It was just as well the passengers could not hear Torquil’s shout or they would have thought the *Queen Mary* was haunted, which of course it was with the four dreamers bring ghosts from the future. This situation meant that the children could wander over the entire ship from bow to stern and they took full advantage of this. Standing on the bows right at the front they felt the liner increase speed as it sailed down the Solent with the Isle of Wight on their right and the City of Portsmouth on the left. Then it was out into the English Channel and the shore was soon left behind with the sea all around and the great ship cutting its way effortlessly through the waves at an ever-increasing speed. This was the first time any of the four had been at sea and even in their dreams they could never have been as thrilled as they were at that moment.

Time now to start exploring the ship, but as they headed for the gangway to go down to the lowest part of the ship Flora said, “I can see land ahead. I didn’t think there would be any land between Britain and America.”

“There isn’t,” said Torquil, “I wonder where that is?” And they were approaching it fast. Closer to land houses and buildings could be seen along the shore and soon a large town came into view and it was here the great liner was heading. “I know the ship is going very fast,” said Morag, “but surely we have not reached America already.”

Soon the *Queen Mary* stopped to be escorted into harbour by the tugboats and the port pilot. As they entered the harbour there was a sign with Cherbourg on it in big letters. “We are in France,” said Calum. “We must be picking up more passengers for the voyage to America." The great ship was edged into a specially built docking berth to take the huge bulk of the *Queen Mary*. Soon a problem became apparent. The access gantries were too short to reach the embarkation points on the ship.

Soon a gang of workmen appeared and a new structure was erected to bridge the gap between the dock and the ship. This was a big setback for the *Queen Mary* on her maiden voyage. At last the work was completed and the transfer of passengers and goods was completed and the tugboats guided the huge liner back out into the open sea.

Once again the excitement of being on the *Queen Mary* and with America the next stop took control, as the discovery of the wonders on this great ship began. It was decided to start at the bottom and work their way through the ship so that no detail would be missed. Once again the freedom of the ship was theirs and no one could see them enter places that were forbidden to the passengers. They headed down the stairways until Flora said, "I think we must be near the bottom of the ocean." Five decks below they reached the engine rooms. No passengers were allowed down here. A strange feeling when exploring was the feeling that they could just walk through closed doors and the walls of the ship, but somehow they felt that this was not polite and they would always wait until a door opened before passing through. In the engine rooms they watched the great engines drive the ship's propellers through the water. The engineers watched all the various gauges and oiled the equipment as they listened to the commands from the control bridge giving instructions. Further towards the stern was another stand-by engine room and beyond that five great boilers providing the steam. Up to the next decks, with interest on every deck, but one deck really took their attention as they entered a swimming pool the likes of which they had never seen. It had diving boards, showers and luxury lounge areas. They spent a lot of time here and being a ghost was a handicap, as they would love to have been passengers and enjoy a swim in this lovely pool.

Up on the busier decks now with people doing much the same as themselves by exploring the ship and another part was reached where being ghosts from the future resulted in them feeling as if they were suffering a kind of torture. Dinner was being served in the cabin class dining room and the temptation of the food was cruel. One thing the four dreamers loved was their food, but never before had they seen such tempting food as that being served in that dining room and they would have to dream their hardest to even imagine a feast like this. The sweets alone would probably have made them sick, but at the moment they were sick because they could not get any of the ice cream, chocolate and fruit delicacies. Morag saw a shelf with menus on it and she read: '*Queen Mary* Maiden Voyage. Dinner menu. 27 May 1936,' This was the first time they knew what time in history they had returned to and this menu was the menu for the day the liner left Southampton on the way to Cherbourg.

The next deck was out into the open again and they felt that they had just witnessed the wonders of the world as they went from deck to deck.

The ship catered for different classes. There was the cabin or tourist class, the lounge cabin class and the staterooms. A thing that struck the children was that everyone regardless of the class, was all very well dressed. The ladies in long flowing dresses and the gentlemen in suits, collars and ties. Only on the sports decks was the formal dress absent. The sporting areas were numerous with tennis courts, bowls and deck games being well used.

As the children started on the four upper decks, Torquil had been counting the lifeboats mounted on derricks along each side of the ship. "There are twenty four lifeboats," he said, "I hope they never have to be used." In the event of this, however, there were evacuation exercises for the passengers and crew, with special areas in each section to head for in an emergency.

The further up the ship they went, the more luxurious it became with beautiful furnishings. If the children were in awe when they had watched the great engines below, the lavish interiors of the upper areas were beyond anything that could be seen in their modern age. There were cabin class restaurants and bars, cabin class smoke rooms, cabin class lounges. The upper lounge smoke rooms, restaurants, bars, drawing rooms, children's play areas and above all the extravagance of the state rooms, that no modern day hotel could hope to match. Indeed the children felt more like being in a huge London hotel rather than on a cruise liner.

Calum spotted on an information desk a leaflet giving details of the ship and he read the following:

The *Queen Mary* is the first ship to be named the same name as the reigning Queen of a country.

The ship was built at Clydebank in Scotland by John Brown & Co. The length of the ship is 1,000 feet. The tonnage 8,237 tons.

Today's speed is 34 knots (39 miles per hour) and the number of passengers on board is 1,805.

Provisions taken on board are:

4,000 gallons of milk
70,000 eggs
11,000 lbs fresh fish
50,000 lbs potatoes and veg.
77,000 lbs meat
2,000 lbs cheese
11,000 lbs sugar
4,000 lbs tea and coffee
1,000 bottles of beer
100 lbs of caviar
15,000 bottles of wines and spirits

It took 43,000 cubic feet of storage for this amount of food.

The ship had four kitchens with 120 kitchen staff.
40,000 meals were estimated for each crossing.

The man with the full responsibility for the *Queen Mary* is Captain Sir

Edgar Britten.

Every night the four dreamers would search the entertainment areas to find the best suited to them and this was usually in the children's lounge class, where clowns and magicians kept them enthralled.

After the ship had been explored from end to end the children took up their favourite spot and this was right at the bow where they had stood on the very first day. Standing here now with the huge Atlantic breakers being sliced through effortlessly by the powerful engines of the *Queen Mary* was the most thrilling adventure they had ever experienced. Although the passengers were not permitted to the front of the ship and they were quite a long way from where the children were standing, an excited murmur from the passengers' areas caused the children to look back and they could see people standing along the decks with binoculars looking straight ahead. Calum stood up on a box and in the far distance he could see land. "I can see America!" he cried, and they all strained their eyes to get a glimpse of land.

The children had no idea of how long they had been sailing. Time was something that never entered their minds. With so much interest every minute it was just a case of what will we see next.

Now that the cruise to America on this great ship was nearly over the memories of this trip would never be forgotten, but a sad thing that kept upsetting them was the fact that when they returned to Strathbrochan they could not tell anyone of their travels.

From the best viewpoint on the ship the four dreamers watched as the *Queen Mary* entered the Hudson River and soon the Statue of Liberty could be seen on the left. The children knew about the statue and how it symbolised the American dream of freedom for all. An air of calm seemed to cover the ship as the passengers looked on to the impressive monument.

Ahead the mighty skyscrapers could now be seen and the air of calm was changed to one of sheer excitement with the expectations of the wonders and magic of this famous city soon to be experienced by the passengers. New York here we come.

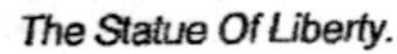

The Statue Of Liberty.

New York Skyscrapers.

Nearing the harbour the ship was surrounded by a fleet of small tugboats and a multitude of other small craft, all with horns and hooters blazing to welcome the greatest liner afloat to New York harbour. This was a welcome that only New York could provide.

High in the sky all around soared the mighty skyscrapers and the children's eyes were riveted on them. Morag's attention was drawn to two exceptionally high buildings that seemed to touch the sky. "I wonder if those two buildings were the ones destroyed by the terrorists on September the eleventh 2001," she said, and the horror of the thought saddened the joy of the trip. "Would it not be wonderful if we could tell the people we see on our trips into the past of the dangers that lie ahead for them in the future?" she continued.

"The trouble is no one would listen," said Calum. "History has already shown that."

Torquil was imagining himself climbing right up on the top floor of the highest building and in his excitement he threw his arm in the air and said, "Imagine working on the top floor of that skyscraper. It would take half a day to get to work." He just got the sentence finished when the four dreamers were surrounded in a mist and when it cleared they were back on the far shores of Loch Brochan. Torquil had let go of Flora's hand in his excitement and we know that this breaks the spell that keeps the dreamers in the visit to the past.

It was disappointing not to have landed in New York, but they were delighted with this trip into the more recent past. Calum said, "We have witnessed five days into the past and have not slept a wink." This was the complete opposite from our terror trip on the Drummossie Muir at Culloden, when Scotland suffered a defeat. This trip has shown how Scottish pride was lifted by this great ship and since then Scottish engineers have been welcomed all over the world. It is a sad state of affairs that the great shipyards of the River Clyde no longer build the great liners of the world and if it was not for the requirements of the Royal Navy there would be no ship building at all.

Torquil said, "I think that this experience has been a wonderful thing for us and we should be very happy with our voyage on the greatest ship the world will ever see. I am sorry I broke the spell by my enthusiasm at seeing those skyscrapers, but we can always visit them again sometime in the future without being ghosts from the past

When the children returned to Strathbrochan they were amazed to find that it was only five o'clock and it was still Thursday. On Friday the thought of the next visit to Loch Brochan was on all their minds, but still there was a worry about the next experience being a frightening one.

The weekend was spent with each of them being involved with their families and a visit to Loch Brochan was not possible. On Monday Calum made straight for the mobile library when it came to search for a book on the *Queen Mary*. He eventually found one telling about the Blue Riband Trophy that used to be awarded to the fastest liner crossing the Atlantic in both directions. He was delighted to read that between 19 and 28 August in 1936 the *Queen Mary* broke the record by sailing westward to America in four days, four hours and 12 minutes. The return sailing eastwards took four days, six hours and 20 minutes. The Blue Riband Trophy was awarded to the *Queen Mary* and this made Calum a very proud boy indeed. The other three dreamers were equally delighted when Calum told them of the award.

This was a fitting end to their great voyage.

6
The Jurassic Age

The following week the time was taken up with school activities and various other things, like having to go with their parents. As always the torment of not being able to tell everyone of the voyage on the *Queen Mary* annoyed the four dreamers, because they knew people would laugh at them.

Unknown to them, however, there was one man in the village who was not sure whether to believe the children or not. The man was Archie Reid. Now Archie Reid was in the same position as the four dreamers, because he could not tell anyone of his experience. On the day that the dreamers had witnessed the meteorite crashing down into the loch, Archie had been trying to net a salmon in the River Brochan quite a long way from the loch. He was standing in the river wearing long Wellingtons, when all of a sudden a huge wave came sweeping down the river and he was drenched right up to his chest. He had netted salmon on this stretch of the river for many years, but he had never known of any large wave like this on the river before. The reason he could not tell anyone in the village was because he always denied being a poacher and he would be found out if the story got out. Hurrying back to his home he took great care to avoid being seen and quickly changed his wet clothing. It was only when the children had told of seeing a huge object crash into Loch Brochan that he realised that the children may actually have seen something and he was always interested in what the dreamers had been dreaming about after that. Maybe they were not all dreams.

It was the following Saturday before the children managed to arrange a trip to Loch Brochan and the excitement was building up in expectation of another trip into the past. Reaching the loch they all clasped hands, the water stirred and the now familiar column of water vapour rose from the loch and they were shrouded in the mist. The mist remained over them for a very long time before lifting. When the mist cleared a strange land stretched out in front of them. It was mostly flat with jagged rocks jutting out of the earth in the distance. There were some deep hollows and the sound of waves could be heard over on their left, where the land seemed to slope down to the sea. There was a strange atmosphere and the daylight did not seem natural. Heavy clouds hung overhead and they seemed to create a feeling of unease. This was an unreal world.

The area where they stood had at one time been a forest as the remains of tree stumps could be seen and it looked as if the trees had just been wrenched from their roots. Tough grass and reed-like plants covered the earth. A deadly silence lay over this land, which could be imagined to be another planet. "Surely we have not travelled through space to some remote planet," said Calum, "because we can breathe easily without any trouble."

"What are we going to do in a place like this?" said Flora.

Torquil said, "There seems to be a forest along the shore. I think we should walk along until we reach it and there may be signs of life there."

It was a long way to the forest and it was not as they had imagined. Some of the trees were enormous, with the remains of shrubs everywhere. The trees were bare, as if some great machine had whisked all the leaves and branches from them.

It began to get dark and the children were wondering why they had been brought to this place. There must be some reason as every previous trip into the past had. It became too dark to enter any further into the forest and so they huddled down at the foot of a large tree to wait for daylight.

After a short time something was moving. Was it a rabbit? No, it was bigger than that, maybe a fox? Surely not a wolf? It could be a deer, but as it came closer it was obvious that this was a huge animal. A crunching sound broke the silence as the animal made its stealthy approach and the dreamers strained their eyes to try and get a glimpse of the creature. Another crunch and the sound was high above their heads. Looking up in the direction of the sound a figure stood out against the slightly lighter shade of the sky and it was very big. Bigger than an elephant and it took an awful long time for it to pass by. There was no way of telling what it looked like. The only thing the children could say was that it was like no creature on earth.

Daylight seemed to take an eternity in coming and when it did a huge gap could be seen where the animal had passed through during in the night. "It must have been some nocturnal animal and it would probably be looking for food. It is just as well we were ghosts from the future or we could have been its dinner," said Calum.

Walking further along the shore the forest seemed to be torn apart for a long way before it looked quite normal, but there was no sign of human life at all. Torquil was just about to suggest breaking their handclasps and returning home when a sudden ear splitting roar changed his mind. Looking into the forest a head could be seen at the top of a tree and it was feeding on leaves and small branches as if it was starving. Peering into the forest a sight never before seen by human beings was there in front of them. It must have been about 80 feet long from its head to the end of a long slender tail. Rather like the shape of a rat's tail. Its body was massive with four solid stumpy legs and each movement it made smashed the trees around it. The four dreamers watched as the animal lumbered on as it fed on the trees. "This must be some kind of dinosaur," said Torquil, "and that means that we are someplace in the world before the Ice Age."

"How do you know before the Ice Age?" said Flora.

Torquil replied, "Well," feeling quite important now, "some people think that it was the Ice Age that caused the extinction of the dinosaurs."

"I wonder how many of these creatures we will see," said Calum, "I wish I had learned more about them. I'm sure I saw a book about them in the library and we should try and remember all the creatures that we see to find a name for them when we return to Strathbrochan."

As they went to walk on the earth seemed to tremble with a series of heavy thuds. The creature feeding on the trees turned round to face another creature similar to itself, but it must have been much heavier as its legs pounded the earth. The creatures collided and a terrific battle took place. It was not as if they were going to eat each other, but fighting for food on the trees. Although there were a lot of trees, it must take many trees to satisfy the hunger of these animals. The battle broke off as suddenly as it had started with the effort seeming to be too much for both of them.

A Battle For Food.

"Let's move on," said Morag. "There must be other creatures like those we have seen and that nobody on earth knows they ever existed." With that they moved on to loud bellows from the animals feeding on the trees again.

"I feel as if we are in Jurassic Park," said Flora.

Further along the shore there was a splashing in the water just in front of them and another strange animal came out of the sea walking on two strong bony legs, with a large strong tail trailing behind it. It also had two smaller legs and it was much smaller than the other two monsters they had seen. As it stood up on its hind legs it must have been about 25 feet tall and it looked like a large lizard. Walking over the sand it entered the forest and started to grind the trees with rows of very strong teeth. Its head reminded Morag of a sea horses head. This trip was providing something that nobody had ever seen, or will ever see again.

The Hydrosaurus

Walking away from the shore and through some long grass a huge jagged boulder lay ahead and it was quite high above the grass. Torquil started to climb the jagged spikes to get a better look and to keep their hands clasped the other three tried to climb up also. They got the fright of their lives when the boulder suddenly rose up and they found themselves on the back of a scaly monster about 20 feet long. Its high spiky back sloped down to a head that tapered down to a sharp nose. At the other end its back swept down to a thick tail with vicious looking spikes protruding from each side. It started to lumber along with the children clinging to the spikes on its back. The animal stopped at an area covered with fleshy fungus vegetation and scooped up the plants into its mouth. The children lost no time in jumping off. Although the children realised that the animal could not feel them on its back, or see them, it was still a frightening experience. Leaving the animal greedily scooping the plants into its mouth they moved on and soon saw another animal some distance ahead of them. It was its grunting that drew their attention to it as it fed on the long grass and shrubs. This was the smallest animal they had seen, but it was still about 15 feet long. Its body looked as if it was armour plated with short metal-looking stubs along its back and a row of spikes along each side of the body stretching right back to a short stubby tail. The head reminded the children of a bull's head, but the whole animal had a lizard like appearance.

Unknown to the four dreamers the animal that the children had the encounter with had finished eating and was coming along behind them. When it saw the creature they were watching it started a charge to attack it and with a sickening crash the two met.

Preparing For Battle.

Their main weapons were their spiky tails and they lashed each other mercilessly until they were both bleeding badly. It was the attacking animal that broke off the fight. It looked very badly injured as it limped off ahead of the children. The victor kept on grazing in the shrubbery as if nothing had happened.

Following the injured animal the four dreamers found it again and it was lying on its side. It must have been mortally wounded in the fight and it looked as if it was dying. As they watched the stricken creature, another smaller and slimmer animal appeared from the forest and approached the dying animal quickly. It had long strong back legs, but its front legs were very short and could be used like arms to handle food. A long wispy tail waved in the air behind it. A long neck supported a very small head that seemed out of proportion with the rest of the body. Standing on its hind legs it would be about eight feet tall.

It immediately attacked the larger animal that made no attempt to defend itself and it fed greedily on the flesh that had been ripped from its side in the battle with the armour-plated creature.

The Law Of The Jungle.

It was not a nice sight to watch and they moved on. "That is the way nature works, one animal is another animal's food, "said Morag.

Calum said, "But have you noticed that the last animal we saw was the only one that ate flesh. The rest were all eating vegetation of some sort and yet they were the biggest creatures. It is amazing the strength those animals get from just eating grass and things."

This made the four dreamers think about how all these great creatures had vanished from the face of the earth and each one of them put forward a reason for this. Calum said, "We saw when we arrived in this land that there were no trees left and when we reached the forest it was being destroyed by the great creatures devouring them. There may be hundreds of these creatures and if they all eat like the ones we have seen there will be nothing left for them to eat in a short time and I think they all starved to death."

Morag said, "I think that some kind of disease spread amongst them like a plague and it wiped them all out, or a disease infected all the plant life and destroyed all the vegetation leaving the animals nothing to eat and they all died of starvation."

Flora said, "I think that as we have seen they all fight each other and through time they have killed each other until there weren't enough of them left to exist. When the vegetarian ones died off the flesh eating ones would have no food except by eating each other until they all died out."

Torquil said, "I think a few things happened. I think that they ran out of food because there were too many vegetarian animals. Since the weather was getting colder the vegetation failed to grow again and this continued until the Ice Age and this would cause the death of all the creatures whether flesh eating or vegetarian."

“We will never know the real reason for the demise of the dinosaurs,” said Calum and they all agreed.

As the children thought about why the dinosaurs had died off snow began to fall. “Let’s be grateful for what we have seen here and go back to Strathbrochan to see if we can learn any more about these monsters,” said Calum. They all agreed and unclasped their hands. The usual mist surrounded them and on clearing they were back on the shores of Loch Brochan.

A visit to the library was going to be a must for all of the children. It was a race at lunchtime on Monday to hunt for a book on dinosaurs and at last one was found with supposed illustrations of the animals that lived in the Jurassic period. It was essential that they all agreed on the names of the creatures they had seen, but they had only to guess at the pronunciation of the names they tried to read.

It was decided that the first monster they had seen munching the trees was a Diplodocus and they could all read the name all right. The dinosaur that started the fight with the Diplodocus was similar to an illustration with the unpronounceable name of Brachiosaurus. The success in finding the names of these creatures made them hunt for the names of the other dinosaurs they had seen more intently and it was decided that the animal Torquil had a ride on, thinking that it was a huge boulder, was a Stegosaurus. The next one to be found was the one attacked by the Stegosaurus, the animal looking as if it was armour plated and had the vicious spikes that were responsible for the death of the Stegosaurus. They all agreed the name of this animal was an Ankylosaurus. The success of finding these names was great and the next creature to find a name for was the flesh eating smaller animal. After a bit of disagreement it was decided that this was a Coelophysis, but the pronunciation gave some problems. That left only one creature to find a name for and that was the lizard like creature that came out of the sea to feed on the bushes. This one was harder to agree on, but finally the name of Hadrosaurus was chosen for it.

It was with sheer delight that the children returned to school and each of them tried hard to pronounce the names of the dinosaurs. Spelling would be a problem if they ever wanted to write about their journeys into the past.

After school their thoughts returned to where the next adventure would be, but sadly the nights were getting dark earlier and there was always some reason to prevent them all being able to meet on the same day. At weekends Morag was enrolled for accordion lessons, as she was keen to be able to play that instrument. Calum was playing for the local boys football team on Saturdays. Flora and Torquil sang with the church choir on Sundays.

The children thought that if they could not go to Loch Brochan for a long time the power of the loch may disappear and they would be left with the memories of past visits. Although these memories would always be cherished and they felt very privileged to have experienced them the urge to continue the trips into the past was too strong and they consulted their diaries to arrange another date. After a lot of ifs and buts, it was decided that another date would be possible before it got dark too early. The following Thursday was pencilled in as a possibility.

7
An African Expedition

Mrs McNab, the mobile librarian, was delighted to have the children so excited and interested in the library books. The thing that puzzled her, however, was the varied subjects the children were showing an interest in. When the craze for reading started it was books on the Old Stone Age, then it was the *Queen Mary* and now it as back to the Jurassic Age. The next time she was talking to Miss McTaggart, their schoolteacher, she would ask if this was related to their class work. No doubt she will be more puzzled when Miss McTaggart tells her that only one of these subjects had been talked about in class and that was the lesson on the Callanish Stones.

The Jurassic Age trip was continually talked about all week by the four dreamers and they were wishing that they hadn't broken the spell when they did and continued on the search for other monsters that must have been around at that time. It was too late now and they could not choose to go back again, as it was just where the power of the meteorite took them that would decide their next destination. Where would that be? That was the next big question on all of their minds and they would find out on Thursday evening, as that night seemed to be clear of anything that could prevent the meeting.

As they left on Thursday immediately after dinner Calum's dad shouted after them, "Remember it is getting dark earlier in the evening now, so make sure you are home early." This would probably be the last trip they could go on this year because darkness would be falling earlier every night, especially when the weather was dull.

On reaching Loch Brochan they lost no time in finally clasping their hands. All eyes fell on the still waters of the loch and then the stirring in the centre of the loch followed by the column of water vapour and it descended over the children like a cloud.

When the mist cleared the country was different from anywhere they had been taken to before. They were standing on the top of a rocky out-crop and as far as they could see the land was covered with very tall grasses and shrubs. The grass was not green, but dried out and more like straw. It was obvious they were in a very hot country, but where could this be? In their former trips there was always a Scottish connection, but this land was very far from Scotland.

They started to walk along what looked like a rough trail through the grasses. Whether animals or humans had made the trail they could not tell. They followed the trail for a long way and the grass was so high they could not see very far. They came to a forested area and by the way the lower braches of the trees were stripped of their leaves, it was obvious that there was some type of animal in this area.

As they walked through the trees they became aware of smoke coming from a clearing ahead and they crept forward expecting to see campers cooking on a camp fire, but as they got closer they saw it was coming from the centre of a strange looking village. There were a number of huts made from the high grasses they had just walked through and they were a peculiar shape. Voices could now be heard in some strange language and the first sight of the people in the village drew gasps from the dreamers. The men they were looking at were jet black and they looked very powerful and fierce. They were wearing large headdresses and were bare to the waist with animal skin skirts. Leaves and beaded objects adorned them. A collection of large beads hung around their necks. The men carried large shields made from the pleated grasses and they were armed with a variety of knives and spears.

Torquil was the first to speak, "We are in Africa." He said, "I think that these people look like Zulu warriors, but they are not as tall as I thought they would be. Probably from some other tribe." They watched the scene in front of them and something was being cooked on the open fire. The thought occurred to the four dreamers that these people could be cannibals and it was just as well that they were ghosts, or they would have been today's lunch. From one of the larger straw huts a man appeared dressed in feathers, plants, beads, bones and it looked like anything he could find was hung on his body. "This must be the witch doctor." said Morag, and as she said this the witch doctor leaned over a women lying on a straw mattress and began to chant as he waved some bones over her head. This continued for some time with the warriors looking on. The witch doctor then took a cup-like object and sprinkled some liquid over the woman. He then poured the remainder into her mouth and that seemed to be the end of the treatment as he returned to the hut he had emerged from. "I would not like to live in those huts," said Flora, "One spark from the fire could set them ablaze."

An African Krall or Village

Thinking that this was not the reason for them being in this land the four passed through the village and came to an area where cattle were feeding. They looked quite domesticated, and they had a large hump on their backs, just behind their necks.

Beyond the village the trail through the grasses was much wider and this must be used by the natives. It led to higher ground where a better view could be seen over the grassland. The grass was shorter in this section and they could see movement away to the left. As they watched a large herd of animals was heading towards them and as they drew nearer they could see that they were some type of antelope. They had long spiky horns and they stopped to feed on the shorter grass. One animal had fallen behind the main group and as the four dreamers watched another animal emerged from the longer grasses. It was slinking along with its body close to the ground and it was going to try and surprise the antelope. Just in time the antelope realised that it was being left behind and as it began to run it caught sight of the other animal. It took to its heels and raced on, but the speed of the other animal cut off its path to re-join the main herd. The other animal was now in plain view and it was seen to be a cheetah. They knew that the cheetah was the fastest animal and that it could run at seventy miles an hour, so they thought that the antelope would be easily caught and killed. They were surprised, however, because as the cheetah picked up its amazing speed to attack, the antelope would suddenly change direction and the cheetah would race on. This continued and although it was a case of life or death it looked as if the antelope was playing with the cheetah. The chase ended unexpectedly when the cheetah suddenly gave up the chase and the antelope raced off to join the herd.

This was a long walk and many different animals were seen on the flat grazing lands. The children claimed seeing elephants, giraffes, buffalo and an assortment of different species of antelope. This type of country was not as expected. The four dreamers thought Africa would be more of a jungle with impenetrable vegetation.

A group of men appeared some way ahead on the edge of a small copse of trees and the children thought they would be warriors from the village, but it was a pitiful scene that confronted them when they reached the group. A row of black men had metal rings round their necks and the rings were joined with chains to form a human chain.

The Slave Traders.

These men were slaves that were being taken to be sold by the slave trader who was dressed in a long cloak that reached down to the ground and his head was bound turban-like with cloth. He carried a whip and at the slightest sign of a slave slowing down he was lashed without mercy. The slave trader had a group of powerful looking natives who also kept hounding the slaves onwards. The four dreamers had heard about the slave trade, but seeing this sorry sight brought home the real cruelty of the slave drivers. Flora began to cry and said, "I wish we had never seen this."

They passed on and the slave traders went in another direction. A change of scenery was welcome as they reached a river and a trail along its bank was followed to a calm section of the river and the children's excitement was raised as they saw hippopotamuses wallowing in the water. They looked completely happy in their environment.

The four dreamers were still puzzled as to why they had been brought to Africa, because there was no particular thing that could be thought of as a great event in history. Surely it was not to witness the slave trade.

Further down the river there was much activity ahead where many men and canoes were in the act of setting off down river. Hurrying along to see what was happening they realised that if this group of people left in canoes they would not be able to follow. On reaching the point where the canoes were leaving from, there were many black natives eagerly working loading equipment into the canoes. The children could see that the equipment was not material that natives would use and wondered who they were working for. How were they going to follow and find the answer to this was the problem. They watched all the canoes leaving and then they noticed that there were spare canoes being towed by the ones already loaded. They quickly jumped into one of them and the whole assembly moved off down river. Where were they going? What will happen next? It was a very enjoyable trip down this river, at times they were sailing through gorges and it was better than following the long trail that they had trekked up until now. Ahead the leading canoes were at the end of this river and entering a much bigger river. When the dreamers entered this river they could see it was very much wider and they could just see the other side. Further down this river it seemed as if there was a cloud hanging over it a long way ahead and the children thought it was rain. The leading canoes stopped and pulled into the side. Some men left the canoes and walked on. When the children's canoe was pulled into the bank they jumped off and tried to catch up with the leaders to see who was leading this expedition. The river was now flowing at a tremendous speed and the reason for this was soon to be realised. This great river suddenly stopped as it cascaded over a waterfall. Not just a small waterfall, but a mile wide river plummeting down for many hundreds of feet into the depths of a ravine. The spray from the surging waters was the reason for the vapour cloud they had seen from further up the river.

The group leading the expedition were staring at the falls and the leader of the group was speaking. He was saying, "This is the greatest sight that I have seen since arriving in Africa and I name these falls The Victoria Falls."

Calum was beside himself with excitement. "That is Doctor Livingstone," he shouted, "the great Scottish missionary and explorer. This is the reason for our trip and again it has a Scottish theme, because Dr David Livingstone was born at Blantyre in 1813."

The four dreamers stared in awe at Dr David Livingstone. They were truly privileged people and this would rate highly on their list of trips into the past.

Remembering Calum's dad's warning to be sure and come home early before it got dark they decided to be satisfied with this trip to Africa and unclasped their hands. The mist from the waterfall was joined by the mist from the past and it descended over the children. When it lifted they were back on the shore of Loch Brochan and the sun was still shining. Back home in Strathbrochan a happy group of four children had a very enjoyable evening.

Monday could not come quick enough for the four dreamers to get to the library and search for a book on Dr David Livingstone. They read about the African natives, the discovery of the Victoria Falls, the slaves and the slave traders. Reading this book took them right back to Africa and they re-lived every minute. The river they sailed down first in the canoes was the Chobe River and the mighty river going over the Victoria Falls was the Zambezi River.

After reading this section of the book Calum, Flora and Torquil went back to school, but Morag went to see Mrs McNab and asked if she could take the book home. "Of course you can," said Mrs McNab, "I am delighted that you are so interested in one of the world's greatest explorers and evangelists. Just bring it back when you are finished reading it."

After dinner that night Morag took the book up to her room and she read about the life of Dr David Livingstone from his birth on the 19th March 1813 at Blantyre, then a small mill town in Scotland, until his death in Africa on 1st May 1873. His body was later taken for burial at Westminster Abbey.

She read about all the different expeditions he had led throughout central Africa. Of his life and family and of his obstinacy when demanding that things should be done his way. Although he achieved many things Morag felt his obsession led him to neglect his family and ruin some friendships he should have respected more. Nevertheless, she admired his courage and determination in many situations. She finished reading the book in bed and only put it down when her mother told her to put the light out and get some sleep.

She put the light out, but sleep was not for Morag this night. Well known as a dreamer Morag had not experienced dreams like she was about to dream tonight. They were more like nightmares.

As her eyes closed she was back in Africa and each expedition was followed in detail because she had been there in her trip to the past. The dreams were very vivid. She could imagine landing in Africa and seeing the snow-like sands on the beaches. The journey to the missionary settlement at Kuraman let her see how Livingstone wanted more commitment from the missionaries at the post and how he decided to move north to Mabotsa. As a doctor he treated the sick at his new missionary post. He was interested in the country around the new mission post and would wander where it was dangerous as there were many wild animals and hostile natives in the area.

The Sculpture Of The Lion Attack At The Livingston Memorial Centre.

On one occasion while walking with his trusted servant, Mebalwe, he was seriously injured when attacked by a lion. He had seen the lion about to attack him and fired at it, but the lion pounced on him and grabbed his arm. Mebalwe shot at the lion, but his gun failed to fire. Grabbing his spear he tried to kill the lion and the lion left David Livingstone to attack Mebalwe. The shots fired by Livingstone then took effect on the lion and it dropped dead. Livingstone's arm never recovered from this injury. Morag was right there watching this in her dream and she was screaming.

She was with Livingstone when wild savages would have killed him and eaten him, but his calm manner would save him and no doubt he would say that God was on his side. On some occasions he would actually work alongside the witchdoctor to try and cure someone. He also risked his life trying to get slaves released and was known to have achieved this. Officialdom was continually approached to try and get slave trading stopped. Cruel slave traders could have killed him easily, but he always managed to carry on.

Health was a big problem in Africa and David Livingstone took seriously ill with malaria and had to be carried on hammocks of straw by his servants and this greatly affected Morag as she watched the great man suffer. After each bout of sickness he would push on and he was the first man to cross Africa from west to east. Morag shared his disappointment when he followed the wrong route on his search to find the source of the River Nile, but on the route he followed he discovered another two lakes that the Geographical Society had no knowledge of.

The following morning Morag was not at school. The ordeal of her nightmare had been so real that she felt ill and tired. Her mother called Dr Nichols and he said a good rest would see her feeling a lot better. She was put back to bed and soon fell into a deep sleep.

When she later met the other three dreamers and told them of her nightmare, they could understand how frightening it must have been to be in the same position as Dr Livingstone, as he faced danger in so many instances. Maybe they should not let their journeys into the past affect them so much, because whatever happened on their visits to the past cannot be undone, or have any effect on their lives today. Except perhaps make them better people.

8
An Old Story

Mrs McNab heard of Morag's nightmare after reading the book from the library on the life of Dr David Livingstone and could not understand why it had affected Morag so badly. Many children had read the book before without being troubled. Of course, Mrs McNab did not know that the four dreamers had actually witnessed Dr David Livingstone's expedition to the Victoria Falls and seen the fearsome tribesmen, the slave traders and the wild animals. Reading this book took Morag right back to Africa and to experience every hazard that had to be overcome by Dr Livingstone. It was no wonder she had a nightmare, but it was no good telling anyone about the trip into the past.

The nightmare was not going to stop Morag going on any more trips into the past, but she would not let the experience affect her so badly again.

Although they had returned in daylight from the trip last Friday it was not long after they returned when the darkness fell and it was decided that they would not go to Loch Brochan any more at night. There were always a lot of chores for the children to do, but a late decision was agreed to make another trip to Loch Brochan on Saturday. This was arranged for two o'clock.

On Saturday as they set out Mr Smith was at the gate of his farm and as the children passed he said, "I've seen you heading for the loch quite a lot lately. Have you found some secret treasure or something there that you are keeping to yourselves?"

"Something like that," said Torquil and farmer Smith just laughed.

"Have you taken up day dreaming now?" he said and shook his head.

The four dreamers carried on to the loch, but they kept a look out in case Mr Smith had followed them. However he was too busy trying to get a cow back into a field.

The usual procedure of clasping hands was carried out and the waters stirred and the children were enveloped in the cloud of vapour. This trip into the past was starting on a lonely rocky shore. A mist was hanging over the sea and the four dreamers were gazing out over the water as the waves came rippling in and this was the only sound. From out of the mist a small boat came drifting in on the tide. It slowly reached the shore and lodged between two rocks. The children thought that it was an empty boat, but as they went over to it a young woman was huddled in the bottom. They did not know what to do as ghosts could only stand and watch. In a short time a man appeared. He was dressed in a long robe of sackcloth and his hair hung down his back.

"Do you think that is Jesus?" said Flora.

"I don't think so," said Calum, "I think that we are somewhere in Scotland and this man is some kind of saint."

When the man saw the girl in the boat he hurried down and helped the girl out. The four dreamers followed as the man took the girl up a path from the shore to a building made with large stones that were built together like a jigsaw without cement binding them. The roof was thatched with thousands of long straw – like grasses tightly bound. They heard the saint say this is a safe place for you to have your child. I would ask you to call the child Mungo if it is a boy.

The four dreamers were expecting something to happen, but what did happen surprised them, because it had never happened before on any other trip. Their hands were tightly clasped and yet a mist dropped down over them. The children thought that when the mist cleared they would be back at Loch Brochan. They were bewildered to find themselves outside a building with a fire blazing inside. There were a number of children running about. They seemed to be going to collect firewood to keep the fire burning. One boy was being bullied by the others and he was continually chased into the woods to get more firewood, while the others played themselves. When darkness fell it was very cold and it was a frosty night. The bullies shouted at Mungo to keep the fire burning till morning and they all went to sleep. The boy Mungo was so tired after running into the woods all day that he fell asleep and the fire went out. When he awoke and saw that he had neglected his duty he had such a strong faith that God would help him to relight the fire. He went outside and took a small frozen branch from a tree. He threw it on the ashes and with a little prayer commanded it to burn. It immediately burst into flame.

Morag said, "This must be the baby that the saint asked the girl to name Mungo, before the mist came over us. The mist must have carried us on to a later stage in the boy's life and this is him in some sort of religious school." This was proved when the saint appeared in the doorway. He had his arm stretched out and a robin was perched happily on his finger.

The bully boys decided to play a wicked trick on Mungo. "Let's kill St. Serf's robin and blame it on Mungo because he is also St Serf's pet." The first time the robin flew near them they threw stones at it and killed it. Mungo found the little bird, lifted it gently and with a few words of prayer he asked for the robin to become alive again. The robin opened its eyes and was soon chirping merrily. The watching bullies were amazed to see this miracle before their eyes and realised that Mungo was greater than any of them. There was no more bullying and Mungo was treated with respect. The four dreamers were amazed at what they had witnessed, but before they could remark on it a cloud of mist enshrouded them again.

When the mist rose a much older Mungo was walking along a lonely country lane. He was heading for an old house and on reaching it the door was opened by a sick old man. "Good morning Saint Fergus," they heard Mungo say. "Are you not feeling well?"

Saint Fergus said, "Mungo I have not long to live. When I die I want you to put my body on the cart and tether two wild bulls to it, drive them on and wherever they stop bury me there."

Saint Fergus died during the next night. In the morning Mungo went out and to his surprise two wild bulls were grazing nearby. It was easier than he thought it would be to get them harnessed to the cart. Saint Fergus's body was placed in the cart and Mungo set the bulls off as requested by Fergus. Mungo and the four dreamers followed the bulls for a long way before they stopped and Mungo buried Saint Fergus at that spot. The children were so interested that not a word had been spoken between them since the mist had lifted.

Mungo stayed at the place where he buried Fergus and hearing that this ground was regarded as holy ground, he build a small church there.

Again the mist descended over them and when it cleared a group of soldiers were hounding Mungo from his church. He was being banished from the land by a cruel king. The four followed Mungo as he wandered far away from his green land and as he walked he would preach to the people on the way and he told them he had been driven from his land that he called Glas Go by the cruel king. Later Mungo was told that the king had been defeated and he returned to Glas Go. The people welcomed him back and helped him rebuild his church.

The four dreamers saw the palace of the new king and they went in to have a look around. The king was on his throne and he was telling his queen that he wanted her to wear the ring he had given her as a present, at the palace ball, which was soon to be held. The children noticed the queen looking very worried and they followed her as she left the room. She headed straight for one of the palace knights and said to him, "You will have to give me back the ring I gave to you because the king demands that I wear it at the palace ball."

The knight just laughed and said, "I am going to keep the ring my lady."

The queen left very distraught and did not know what to do.

The four dreamers went back to see what the knight was going to do, but he had been summoned to attend a meeting of all the knights. The children realised that the king knew the queen had given the ring to this knight and at the meeting with the king there was a lot of wine drunk and the meeting lasted well into the night. When the knight with the ring fell asleep the king took the ring from his finger. It was obvious that the king wanted rid of his queen and he was going to use the ring as an excuse. The four dreamers followed the king and saw him throw the ring into the river. How would the queen ever get the ring back now? She knew the king would destroy her.

The next day the children were watching Mungo at his church when the queen arrived dressed in ordinary clothes. She told Mungo of her plight and asked for his help. Mungo called a monk and told him to go to the river and fish. "Bring the first fish you catch to me," he said. The monk caught a fish with his first cast and brought it back to Mungo. He opened the fish's mouth and there was the queen's ring and she would be able to wear it at the palace ball. The queen happily thanked Mungo for what she considered to be pure magic.

When the queen left a messenger arrived with a large box for Mungo. Mungo was surprised at receiving a present and on opening the box there was a huge bell inside. There was a message saying that it was a present from his superiors in recognition for his work in establishing a new church. Mungo wasted no time in having the bell installed and he was a happy man.

The four dreamers were deep in thought over the things they had seen during this trip into the past. Calum said, "Most of what we have seen has been like a legend, rather than fact unlike the other trips we have been on. I think that this is the past of a legend rather than a real life happening."

Morag was the cleverest at history and she had been connecting all the things they had witnesses on this strange trip. She said, "I know that Saint Mungo is the patron saint of Glasgow and that he is buried in Glasgow Cathedral and that part of our trip could be reality." She also said, "Glasgow's coat of arms has the bird that never flew, the tree that never grew, the bell that never rang and the fish that never swam, but we have seen the little robin flying, the tree was growing, Mungo's bell was rung and the fish was swimming before it was caught. I think we can take the bird, the fish, the tree and the bell as legend and sprinkle the rest with truth and fiction. What we really saw was the birth of the city of Glasgow."

9
The Invaders

It was now mid-September and the chances of the four dreamers meeting at the same time was getting more difficult. Calum was now playing football for the local juvenile team. Morag was taking lessons on playing the accordion. Flora was attending highland dancing classes. Torquil went with Calum to the football and he was hoping to join the team also. This left Sunday as the only free day and the children had to attend junior church in the morning.

The first Sunday afternoon that all the children were free and the weather was fine a hurried meeting resulted in the decision to head for Loch Brochan. Reaching the loch the now normal procedure of clasping hands, searching for the water to stir and the mist descending over them took place as expected.

The mist lifted and there was panic all around. The people from a small village were leaving their homes and heading up a glen into the hills. They were carrying whatever they could and a man was shouting, "The Vikings are coming, flee for your lives!" As the children watched the few houses in the village were now empty and a silence fell over the area.

The small village was at the end of a long loch and it was from further down this loch that the Vikings had been seen. The reason for the panic became very clear as a fleet of Viking longboats came sailing into view. Reaching the village the sails were lowered and the longboats hauled up onto the shore. The Viking warriors raced up into the village and began to raid the houses taking whatever they thought might be useful to them. The soldiers wore armour and carried mighty swords. They searched for the villagers in vain and it was fortunate that the villagers had been warned. They had now fled up the glen and reached the safety of secret caves high up the rocky hillside.

Attacking this village was not the reason for the Viking invasion. They settled down in the village for the night to eat and rest. At first light they were up and stout ropes were attached to the longboats. Teams of soldiers grabbed the ropes and the boats were hauled up from the shore. Some Vikings went to a forest and chopped down some trees. Branches were stripped off and the trees were used as rollers to make it easier to haul the longboats over difficult sections. There was a low valley between the hills on the opposite side of the village from the glen the villagers had fled up and this was where the longboats were being dragged.

Calum said, "These Vikings seem to know the country. They must have planned this raid and this army is invading to a plan." There were hundreds of soldiers and the boats were hauled over the grassy fields. The tree trunks were used to free the boats when they got stuck.

A Viking Long Ship.

The children followed the boat haul and it was not long before a stretch of water was seen ahead. When this was reached the longboats were launched into the water and the Vikings rested after the strenuous task they had just carried out. The longboats must have been dragged about two miles overland.

The rest period did not last long and the commanders ordered the soldiers into the longboats. The boats started to sail down this inland loch and the four dreamers had to run to jump into a boat carrying supplies. It was a long sail down the loch and when settlements were seen along the shore the Vikings would land and pillage the houses and farms.

At the end of the loch the Vikings moored the boats and each man was loaded up with arms and supplies and they formed up to march on. They definitely had a plan and it seemed that time was of the utmost importance. The children followed behind. "I think the Vikings are going to attack Stirling Castle," said Torquil. "I think that was Loch Lomond we have just sailed down and in the olden days the Kings of Scotland would be living in Stirling Castle. These Vikings are going to try and conquer Scotland."

It was a very daring plan and this was why they were in such a hurry, as a surprise attack would not be expected from this side of the castle.

It was a very long march and the soldiers were tiring. At one point Stirling Castle could be seen in the far distance and the land looked flat all the way to Stirling. This gave the Vikings renewed energy and they pushed on faster.

Unknown to the Vikings they were heading for a treacherous place and it was Morag who said, "I have read about the Romans occupying this land and it was then heavily forested. This allowed the ancient Picts to hide in the forest and raid the Romans and steal their supplies. The Romans decided to cut down the whole forest and burn the trees. This took away the Picts cover and the raiding stopped. Cutting down the trees caused the remnants of the forest to rot and rain soaked into the rotten wood and the area could not dry out. This over hundreds of years created an impenetrable bog that no-one could cross over." The Viking army were now heading for this area and this must have been unknown to them when they planned this attack.

Suddenly there was panic from the Viking army as it landed in this bog. The soldiers were so heavily laden that they sank in the bog and the more they struggled the quicker they went down. The commanders realised too late what was happening and ordered the soldiers back, but this was not possible and many men disappeared into the bog. The army was now greatly weakened and not the mighty fighting force that had arrived in Scotland.

Scouts were sent out to find a way round the bog, but by the time this was done the screaming of the men being sucked into the bog had been heard a long way off and the army at Stirling Castle had been alerted and were put on guard.

When a new route was found the remaining Vikings continued to march to Stirling, but they were seen from the castle and a huge Scottish army lay in wait for them. A battle took place and this reminded the children of Culloden, but this enemy was defeated and many of their soldiers were drowned in the River Forth. The Vikings tried to retreat to their boats on Loch Lomond, but this route was cut off by soldiers from Stirling. The commander then ordered his army to retreat westwards to reach the west coast and they were chased all the way. This was a difficult part for the four dreamers who were trying to keep up with the Vikings and keep their hands clasped at the same time. Finally the west coast was reached and the Vikings took up defensive positions. It was then something that must have been known to the Viking commander happened. A large fleet of Viking ships came sailing up the coast with another Viking army to reinforce the weakened army. The Scottish army attacked immediately and so quickly that the Vikings had no time to link up their forces and they were driven back. The ones that survived the Scottish onslaught fled to their longboats and sailed away.

The four dreamers were not affected so much this time at seeing a battle because it was not such a brutal massacre as the Culloden battle and the enemy were defeated. Feeling that this trip was now over the dreamers unclasped their hands and the mist appeared to return them to Loch Brochan.

Once again it was a race to the library on Monday and the history books were eagerly read. The story of what they had seen was explained. In the year 1263 King Haaken of Norway sent his son Prince Olaf with a huge army to take the Scottish king, Alexander the Third, by surprise. This army sailed up Loch Long and landed at the village now called Arrochar and hauled their boats over to Loch Lomond at a place called Tarbet – this name is derived from the gaelic word meaning boat haul, as the four dreamers had seen and they sailed on to attack Stirling. The children knew the result of that and the following victory for King Alexander the Third.

The battle with the Vikings was called the 'Battle Of Largs' and a monument there commemorates the battle. The monument is nicknamed 'The Pencil' due to its shape resembling a pencil.

10
City Visit

There was usually a children's outing to a pantomime in either Edinburgh or Glasgow, but this year the day out was to visit some of Glasgow's attractions. There was a committee in the village and Colonel and Lady Maxwell were very much involved in anything the committee proposed. The cost of such outings and other events was funded from raffles and social evenings. Any event run by the committee was always very well organised.

The next outing was arranged for the first Saturday in October and Calum thought that he would not be able to go because of the football, but there were so many players wanting to go on the outing that it was agreed to postpone the match for that Saturday. It was going to be a long journey and the bus was leaving at eight o'clock.

The big day arrived and children and parents were up early. The women of the village had prepared sandwiches, made scones and cakes, as it was to be a picnic lunch. Angus McGregor provided crisps, biscuits, sweets and drinks for use on the bus. The bus left prompt at 8 o'clock as everyone was there early and the journey to Glasgow was uneventful. The first place to be visited was the Museum of Transport which had been relocated at the new Exhibition Centre. It was a full-time job for the adults to try and control the children. Once inside the children ran to the exhibits that caught their attention and they were spread all over the hall in minutes. The old methods of transport had them in wonderland, as they saw the first horse-drawn trams with open top seating. Then the old tramcars with their different colours as each route had its own colour. The next stage was the luxury coronation class trams in cream, orange and green. Round on to the old railway carriages and then the real favourites. The steam locomotives looked massive and majestic, as if they were proud to be on display and that they were built in Glasgow. It was a reminder of when Glasgow built the locomotives for the rest of the world. The four dreamers were going round with their parents, but as everyone was admiring the display each of the dreamers were in their own dreamlands. As Calum stared at these great locomotives he was in the wild west of America with raiding parties of Indians racing alongside with rifles blazing and he was with the soldiers defending the train as it sped through the hostile land. The party moved round to the motorcar section. The old cars produced in Scotland were very interesting as were all the cars on display. Torquil was miles away as he stared as a replica of a James Bond car and he was racing along a narrow twisting mountain road, bringing all the gadgets of the films into play as he was attacked by motor cyclists and helicopters with rockets and bullets whizzing around him. They moved on now to the old horse-drawn coaches that were the only form of transport in the olden days. Morag was a lady of importance and dresses in the most fashionable finery and wearing priceless jewels as she was being driven to a ball. Suddenly pistol shots were being fired and highwaymen held up the coach. The coach door was thrown open and she was robbed of all her lovely jewellery. Then it was on to the display of the old fairground and travelling folks caravans of bygone years. Flora was lost in her dreams as an old lady sitting in front of a crystal ball told of things that would happen to her in the future. She was going to marry a handsome prince and live in a fine castle with servants and handmaidens at her beck and call.

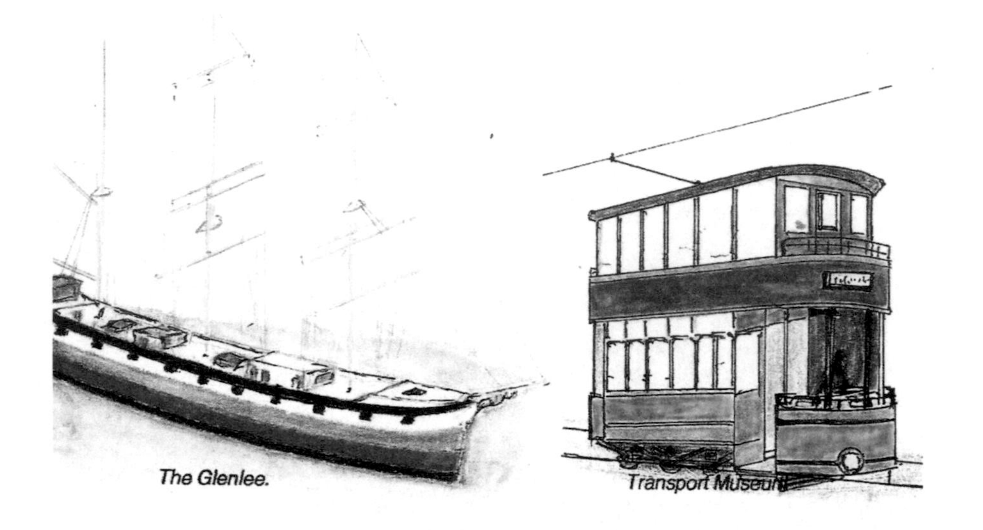

The Glenlee. *Transport Museum*

Next it was upstairs to the creation of the bicycle and the motorcycle with each bringing on dreams of being a champion racer. The model ships section raised a lot of excitement, as the workmanship required to make the models was admired and the children could imagine voyaging to distant lands in these great ships. When the four dreamers saw the model of the *Queen Mary* they were not dreaming, but remembering every moment of their trip into the past. Returning to the main entrance there was a side street built as an exact copy of an old Glasgow street. There were old shops with the goods of bygone years displayed in the windows. The first type of carriage used on the Glasgow underground is in a mock up of the typical subway stations of that time. An old cinema was a favourite with some of the adults who could remember the times shown on a film of old Glasgow.

The children were all collected to ensure no one was missing and this was a problem with children wanting to buy souvenirs before they left. It was then out on to the bus and a drive round to Kelvingrove Park. If the weather was fine it was picnicking in the park and if it had been wet it would be lunch on the bus. This was a fine day and it was a lovely place to have lunch, with Glasgow University looming on one side and the Glasgow Art Galleries on the other. The picnic was wonderful and the sandwiches and baking enjoyed by all. The children managed to keep some scraps and had fun feeding the pigeons.

The next place for a visit was the *Glenlee* sailing ship moored at Glasgow Harbour on the River Clyde. The entrance to the ship is through an old pump house, which is a listed building and now the reception hall, where posters and videos give relevant facts on maritime history. While the adults watch the videos there are desks with various pastimes for the children. The four dreamers were attracted to a model of the *Lusitania* built by John Browns on the Clyde in 1907. What interested them was the reference to the Blue Riband Trophy, which it won in 1908. They remembered the *Queen Mary* winning the trophy in 1936. Reading the history of the ship told of it being torpedoed off the coast of Ireland by a German submarine in 1915 and 1,195 people died – a devastating loss at that time.

From this point it was out on to the harbour and the *Glenlee* lay ahead of them. Before they had even boarded the ship their minds were racing and their imagination took control. No longer was this an old ship restored as a museum piece to one of the last sailing ships still afloat and built in Glasgow, but a fully sailed ship sailing on the high seas in search of fortune. Racing up the gangway the huge ship's bell had a rope dangling from it and it was too much temptation and it rang out quite a number of bells in record time. The huge anchor chain and the machinery to operate it drew gasps of surprise. Then up on to the prow and to ring the bell and then gaze out over the bowsprit. Going down the stairs the crews sleeping quarters were wooden frames with hammocks slung across the frames and they lined each side of the room. Flora was staring at them and imagining the ship rolling in a storm and the hammocks swinging about.

"I could never sleep in those beds," she said.

There was a lot of information regarding the restoration work that was required to bring the *Glenlee* into her present condition and this was more interesting to the adults than the children. The size of this vessel is deceiving. From the outside it does look very big, but when down in the cargo holds it is enormous and there are samples of the cargo it used trade in such as grain, timber, sugar, wool and whatever goods that could be traded on any particular voyage.

A large map showed the trade routes this ship had sailed although not always under the same company. It also had a name change to the *'Islemount'* at one time.

The children wandered in their usual land of dreams. Actually not their land if dreams, but their ship of dreams. Calum was away with the pirates when he saw the skull and crossbones flag and he was sailing the seven seas raiding and boarding the merchant vessels with cutlass drawn with his band of pirates looting and pillaging. He was Blackbeard for a day. It is probably just as well he was dreaming because the *Glenlee* carried no guns – just black painted squares to pretend to pirate that the ship was heavily armed.

Torquil was the captain of a trading ship collecting cargo and sailing the stormy seas under sail and discovering new lands to become as famous as Captain Cook.

Flora could imagine the cargo deck packed with slaves all chained together. They were being taken from Africa just like the ones she had seen when following David Livingstone on their trip into the past and they were going to be sold in America.

Morag imagined her father was the captain of this ship and he was taking the family on a world voyage. No thoughts of pirates or sea battles just pure luxury on this great sailing ship, but at the back of her mind was what it would be like in a storm and being tossed about in the sea like a cork in the water. This brought her back to reality and she thought, I like it better just walking through the ship and admiring what it had achieved as the *Glenlee*.

The route through the ship came to the poop deck at the stern, where the captain and the officers' quarters were. There was a great steering wheel and the children could imagine the sailors trying to keep the ship on course in a gale. From the stern they walked along the top deck and the three huge masts soared high overhead with all the rigging and spars that the sails would have been attached to. Amidships there was the ship's galley and a not too appealing crew's dining area. This brought the tour of the ship back to the gangway and it was back on shore to head for the bus again. This had not been a long visit, but it was enjoyed by all.

The next place to be visited was the new Science Centre and the children felt that they had travelled into the future. The shape of the buildings was like something from outer space. Across the river Clyde was the Armadillo, named because of its shape. This was the Clyde Auditorium. The shape of the science building was something similar and the Imax cinema complex was like a huge balloon on water. The tallest building in Glasgow - the only revolving tower in Europe, dwarfed both buildings.

Entering the large reception area the children were eager to see what was interesting and the parents had their work cut out to keep them in an orderly group until the tickets were purchased and it was decided who was going where. It was then up the elevator to the first floor and never had the children, or the parents seen so many gadgets, games and things to try out. Everything was demonstrating some particular science, but this was of no concern to the children who just raced around trying one thing after another. It was pure science made entertaining. This form of science elitism continued up for another two floors – it was pure magic.

The Glasgow Science Park.

The four dreamers were then taken up the tower. They had to go down a long passage that took them down to the base of the tower and all the machinery to operate the tower was explained to the adults. The tower was sitting on a large ball bearing and the electric motors that turned the tower were spaced around the base. The motors were not controlled by an operator but by the wind and this enabled the tower design to be facing the correct way into the wind. The tower would be closed to the public in severe weather. There were films about the growth of the City of Glasgow in three stages before the lift took the children to the top of the tower. The views were magnificent all around Glasgow and many well-known landmarks could be picked out. The tower was continually turning one way then the other as the wind changed direction. The lift arrived again and took them back down to join the others still playing with the gadgets. If the children understood all the technology that was involved in the creation of these amusing gadgets, they would leave here today junior scientists. As would the parents.

It was now time to go to the IMAX cinema for what would be the highlight of the day. As they entered they were given glasses with one lens green and the other red. When the film started they wore the glasses and the objects on the screen seemed to be zooming out of the screen. The film was about travelling to outer space and there were rockets and spacecraft whizzing all around the cinema. No dream could compare with this and the children thought they were actually taking part in the film.

This was the end of the day's outing except for a high tea arranged at a Glasgow restaurant and the end of a perfect day. There were a lot of sleepy children on the long drive home and there were more than four dreamers on that bus.

When the four dreamers met the next day they talked about the outing and they thought, what was the difference between them imagining things and what they saw on a visit to the past. They decided that when they were under the influence from the power of the loch they could do nothing but break their clasped hands. While on this visit to the past they were in charge of what they wanted to do.

11
Cold Comfort

Nothing particular happened in Strathbrochan and normal village life carried on in its usual leisurely fashion through the months of October and November, the highlights being Halloween and Guy Fawkes night and these two events give the children an interest up to the next important time of the year that is Christmas and New Year. Both are celebrated in style at Strathbrochan. There are always a number of Christmas parties arranged and carol singing around the village was as much part of Christmas in Strathbrochan as Santa Claus. New Year was also celebrated with the traditional first footing and family gatherings.

The month of January was normally the worst month of the year and this year was no exception. There was a very cold spell with severe frost at New Year and everything was frozen over. As the schools were on holiday the four dreamers decided they would take a walk and wrapped up snugly in their warmest clothes they headed for Loch Brochan to see if the power of the meteorite or comet still worked with the loch frozen over. As they stood on the bank snow began to fall lightly. They clasped hands and stared across the loch. There was not a movement anywhere and they realised that there would be no trip into the past that day.

They decided that they would go for a walk and they headed for Creag Hill on the other side of the loch. The snow was very light and they were not feeling cold in their warm clothes. The walk was very enjoyable and they reached the hill and climbed the five hundred feet or so to the top. As they looked down over the loch they could see that very black clouds were coming over from the direction of Strathbrochan and the village seemed to be disappearing in a mist. They were soon to find out that it was not a mist, but a snow blizzard raging over the village and it was heading towards them. They started to hurry down the hill, but the blizzard hit them before they were halfway down. They struggled on down, but it was hard to see where they were going and the snow became so heavy everything turned white. This was what is called a white out and all possible landmarks that would indicate the direction to go are blanked out with a white curtain. It was not long before the snow was inches deep and the wind was blowing it into deeper drifts. The four dreamers were struggling on, but the worst thing that was happening was that the children had lost all sense of direction and they were heading away from Strathbrochan into remote rough country and the snow was getting heavier. The children realised they must be going the wrong way and tried to change their route, but they were just wandering wildly with no idea where they were.

The snow was now six inches deep and difficult to walk through especially in the deep drifts. Calum said, “We have been walking now for hours and we are lost. I think that we should stop and build a shelter with the snow and keep as warm as we can until help arrives.” There was an old stone wall they thought they could shelter against and then Torquil noticed a hut just beyond the wall, probably used by a shepherd at some time. They made their way over to it and forced open a badly fitting door. It was a relief to get out of the wind and snow.

Morag said, "Our mothers and fathers will be worried about us and they will call out the mountain rescue to look for us."

"My mother will be raging. I will be in real trouble when I get home," said Flora.

"It will be me that gets the blame for getting us lost because I am the oldest," said Calum.

"It was nobody's fault," said Torquil, "we were not to know the snow was going to be so heavy."

"If this snow lasts all night we will be covered with snow in the morning and it will be very hard to find us," said Morag. There were no windows in this old hut and it was in a terrible state. It looked as if someone had been using it as there were wooden planks laid out to form seating and some plastic bags that food had been carried in. When darkness fell it was cold and the children began to shiver. Calum said, "We better try to keep warm, let's jump about or run around the hut until we get heated up and then we can try and get some sleep. They huddled together on the wooden seat and they were so tired that they did manage to sleep for a time.

In the village the children were not missed until after five o'clock. This was when Flora's mum thought Flora would be round in Morag's house. She knew the children were going for a walk, but thought that they would have returned when the snow came on and it was usual for them to be in some of their friend's houses. She phoned round to Morag's house, but Mrs Stewart thought she was in Flora's house because of the snow. "Maybe they are in Calum's house," she said and then she phoned Mrs Alexander's, but of course she had not seen them either. "I will try Torquil's house. They sometimes go there to watch telly." Mrs McPherson said she had not seen them since they said they were going for a walk. The snow was still raging and the other friends of the children were phoned. Nobody had seen the children since they had gone for that walk. Their fathers would normally have been home from work, but they were being held up by the snow affecting the roads. Mrs Walker phoned the police and Sergeant Menzies said that a search would be started immediately. He knew the children well and said, "They are intelligent kids and I don't think they will do anything stupid. He phoned the mountain rescue and the members were called to organise a search. Where were they last seen and where were they going? That was the question. Mr Smith the farmer saw them before the snow came on heading for the path to Loch Brochan. He never saw them coming back because he had been working in the barn. The snow was now very serious and it was keeping the mountain rescue team from being assembled. The children's fathers did not get home until around seven o'clock and Mr McPherson, Mr Alexander, Mr Walker and Mr Stewart gathered warm clothing, flasks of hot tea and food and headed for Loch Brochan. It was a difficult journey and they were soon met by the mountain rescue team. They reached the loch and it was completely covered with snow. It was decided to split the search with some going round the loch to the left and the others to the right. There was a small plantation on the other side of the loch and it was thought the children might be sheltering in the forest. It took hours for the search parties to get round the loch and they were shouting the children's names, but were met with silence. Joe Cameron, the mountain rescue team leader, said, "When the snow is like this it covers everything white and it is almost impossible to find directions without a compass and I think this is what has happened to the children. It was a sudden storm and they would have been taken by surprise. They could have wandered in any direction and we have no idea where they could be." He said he would call the helicopter search team and if the blizzard eased up they were the only hope of finding the children. It was pointless for them to wander about in this deep snow and they all returned to the village.

At first light the wind had dropped and the helicopter search team started a systematic search of the area.

In the hut the children awoke cold and hungry. Calum had them on their feet immediately dancing and running about to warm up. "We must keep warm," he said. "I know someone will find us, but they will have a difficult job and we must not give up." When they felt warmer they sat down and fell silent. Torquil was just about to say the snow is off when the sound of a helicopter made them jump as it passed overhead.

Morag said, "They will have found us with a thing that can seek out heat and they will come and get us." They waited for the helicopter to return, but it kept on going.

Torquil said, "This hut has a corrugated iron roof and it must have a few feet of snow on top. I don't think the heat sensor would detect us through that and they are still searching."

Calum said, "We will listen and if we hear it coming back we will have to rush out and wave our arms to attract their attention." The search team of the mountain rescue and every available man were out searching first thing in the morning. Several parties were operating and each took a different direction, keeping in touch with mobile telephones where the reception was available. In some areas the hills kept the signals from getting through. By now the lost children were being mentioned on television and it was now a national story. Strathbrochan village was now known throughout Britain.

The mountain rescue got a message from the helicopter telling them that they could find no trace of the children on the first search run. This information was a bad thing because the search area covered by the helicopter was cut off the search area on the ground thinking that if the children had been in that area the helicopter would have found them.

The search continued throughout the day and hope of finding the children alive was fading. The search parties met again to think of another plan. Joe Cameron the search leader asked the searchers if they knew any place where the children could have found shelter, like a cave. As they all thought of walks they had gone in the hills, no one could think of any place the children could have found refuge. Archie Reid said there was an old hut on the other side of Creag Hill, but it was very far away and he thought it was too far for the children to have reached it in the snow. He did not mention that he had used it from time to time when stalking deer. Joe Cameron also thought it would be too far away for the children to have reached it and it was well out of the search area, but he said, "We must try every possibility. He got in touch with the helicopter and asked them to fly over this area again and told them the location of the hut. The helicopter headed for the hut immediately.

The four dreamers were now feeling very cold, tired and hungry and their exercising was making them more tired. "We are not going to be found." Cried Flora and Torquil said, "Don't say that, we will be found."

Morag shouted, "Listen!" They all listened and they could hear the helicopter coming back.

"Let's get out and wave," said Calum and they forced themselves out into the deep snow and they could see the helicopter coming. They waved their arms with all the strength they had left and soon the helicopter was hovering above them. As it dropped lower the frozen snow did not blow about too much, but the helicopter could not land for fear of getting stuck in the snow. The children sheltered from the wind set up by the whirling rotors and watched as a man was being winched down to them. The man was as excited as the children at finding them looking quite well and he told them he was going to take them up into the helicopter one by one and Flora was the first to be secured into a harness. A signal was given to the helicopter and Flora was lifted up into the helicopter. The winch was lowered again and Morag was next to be lifted followed by Torquil and then Calum. The cold and hunger was forgotten at that moment. The thrill of being rescued by helicopter seemed to make the whole experience worthwhile. The helicopter crew had hot drinks and food in the plane and they were thoroughly enjoyed.

The search parties waited anxiously for a report back from the helicopter and when they heard the pilot say "The four children are now safely on board and they are well." The cheers could be heard for miles. They all hurried back to Strathbrochan and waved to the helicopter as it flew over them.

When the helicopter landed in the centre of the village square in Strathbrochan the whole village was out to greet the rescuers and the children. The children were hugged by their parents and Flora need not have worried about her mother giving her a hard time and they were all treated like heroes. When the search party returned Joe Cameron said, "The children were amazing. To get lost in those conditions could have happened to experienced climbers. To take shelter and remain there just keeping warm was the right thing to do. If they had tried to walk back to the village they would have wandered further away and the end could have been much worse. Calum was congratulated as the other children said he was the one who saved them. Archie Reid got a cheer all to himself.

The Helicopter Rescue.

12
Pastimes and Disaster

It took many weeks for Strathbrochan to return to normal. The four dreamers enjoyed the limelight with people from the press and television asking about their ordeal in the snow. The worries about not being found and perishing in that old hut were nearly forgotten, but they always had the feeling that they were lucky indeed to be rescued and that lift into the helicopter will be remembered for ever.

The long cold winter lasted well into March before the lengthening daylight hours brought thoughts of spring and soon the weather improved to give some lovely days. The four dreamers had only one thought in mind and that was to get back to Loch Brochan and see what mysteries of the past would be revealed to them.

The Easter holidays could not come quick enough and the four dreamers headed for Loch Brochan on the first day of the holiday that suited all of them and this was Saturday. On reaching the loch their hands were tightly clasped and they gazed across the waters in expectation. They were not disappointed as familiar stirring of the waters produced the cloud of water vapour that swirled over them and they were once again travelling through time.

The mist cleared and the children were in a small village. A very old village. The houses were all made from the same stone and they were in rows built around a central square. There was smoke spiralling up from the many chimney pots. In the square there were two large buildings. One was a school and the other was in a rundown state and seemed to be a place where people lived in dormitories. The tall steeple of a church could be seen at the end of the village and there seemed to be only one shop that served as an inn or public house. The streets were very rough with no hard surface just a sort of hard packed ash and gravel. There were no streetlights.

The four dreamers went into the school and the children were split into two classes. Going into the first class, one look at the teacher made the dreamers glad that they were not in this class. She was a big woman with her hair pulled back and tied in a huge plaited bun at the back of her head. She was dressed in black and her long skirt almost touched the floor. She had a pointer in one hand and she was shouting at a timid little boy, “If you cannot do this lesson as I taught you I will give you the strap. Now give me the correct answers as I point to the number.” There was a large clock face on the blackboard with the numbers 1 – 12 round the face. In the centre was the number eight. As the teacher pointed to the numbers on the clock face the boy had to multiply each number by eight. The boy started off well, but as the teacher started to point to each number quicker he started to make mistakes. “Come out here boy,” the teacher shouted, and reaching into her desk brought out a long leather belt with fingers cut at one end and a handle at the other. “Hold out your hand,” and as she did so she seemed to take great delight in smacking his outstretched hand with the belt. The looks on the faces of the other children in the class was one of fear as they waited to see who would be next to be called out to do the eight times table. Another boy was called out and could not do much better than the first boy. "Come out here boy!" the teacher yelled and as the boy went out in panic he accidentally knocked over a vase of flowers that were on a table next to the teacher's desk. The teacher went wild over this and this time it was not the belt she went for but a long slender cane. "Bend over boy!" and as the boy was leaned over a desk to receive a whack from the cane across his bottom she shouted, "You clumsy boy." Any further punishment for that afternoon was over as a bell rang and that was school over for the day.

The children stood up at their desks and a short prayer was said before they escaped to the playground and home. The boys were wearing caps and most of them had course grey clothing that looked the same. Under their jackets they all had high collared jerseys and their trousers were worn to down below their knees. The girls clothing was just as drab as the boys and their skirts were very long. Most of them had their hair plaited and it hung down their backs in tails.

The Wicked School Teacher.

The four dreamers were amazed at what they had seen. This could never happen at their school and Mrs McTaggart was an angel in comparison with the demon teacher of this class. Following the children out of school the dreamers wondered what the children would do for entertainment or play at. As the children came out of their homes they were changed into older clothes. There was no such thing as a radio or television. What would they do? The girls were the first to start playing and Morag and Flora were really interested. Skipping ropes was the first game and the things those children could do when skipping was amazing, as they jumped in and out, sometimes two at a time and every game they played was accompanied by them singing a catchy little song. Another set of girls was playing on an area of flat stone. The ground was marked out in squares with numbers scratched out in each square. A flat marble stone called a peever was then hit from square to square while hopping on one foot. The hopping foot was the one used to hit the peever. The object of the game was to hit the peever into every square without it landing on a line and without a break in the hopping. Some were also playing with balls being bounced against a wall from many different positions and at times using two balls and all these games were played to the singing of their little songs. The boys were playing in groups at first. One group was shouting 'Hunch, Cuddy, Hunch'. One boy would bend his head down and stoop while another boy leaped over him and he would bend down and the next boy leaped over these two and he bent down the last boy would leap over these three and then it was the first boy's turn to leap over the other three and the game was continued getting faster every time. Those boys were very fit. Some were playing marbles, but not just rolling them along the ground to hit their opponent's marble. They would put a number or marbles each into a group against a wall and standing back about six feet they would throw a steel ball a little bigger than the marbles from many different positions. Each position had a name something like stoogy, periwinkle or double periwinkle. If they managed to hit the marbles they would keep the ones knocked out from the bunch. A similar game was also played where a ring was scratched on the ground and the marbles were placed in the ring. The object of this game was to knock the marbles out of the ring from different positions and they kept the ones knocked out of the ring.

These games were played very seriously and it was a disaster when someone lost all their marbles. Others were playing peeries. The peeries were made of wood. They were about three inches long and circular with grooves cut around them. The top groove was deeper than the rest. The top was flat and the bottom tapered down to a point where a steel pin was fitted to allow the peerie to spin easily. A leather thonged whip was used to make the peerie spin. The fine leather thong was wound round the deep groove at the top and as it was pulled sharply away the peerie would spin and it was kept spinning by whipping it with the whip. The top of the peerie had colours on it and this gave a striking design as the peerie spun. The game was played with several peeries spinning and as they touched each other one would spin off. The peerie remaining spinning at the end was the winner.

When the above games finished team games were played and a favourite was called 'Leavo'. Two teams were picked with mixed boys and girls. An area was marked out and called a den. One team was allowed a certain amount of time to run off and then the other team would give chase. When they caught someone they would bring them back and put them in the den and someone would then be put on den guard. When all the opposing team were caught it was their turn to do the chasing. However, if one of the team being chased could evade capture and run through the den shouting 'Leavo' all of his team that had been caught were set free and had to be caught again. This was a really exciting game to watch. The boys' favourite game was of course football. It was obvious this was a poor village and the boys could not afford a real football. The old type of football was made of leather with an inflatable inner tube. The boys had managed to get an old leather outsider and stuff it with papers to make it round. This was also a very serious game.

As the four dreamers watched all of these games being played in such a friendly way in spite of the hard life those children had in comparison to theirs, they could not help wondering who were enjoying their lives most, because they had never had the thrill or enjoyment that these children were having. Watching television or playing computer games could never give the satisfaction of making their own entertainment and these children looked very fit, although there were some children who looked as if they were suffering from some illness and could not join in the games. The games they had watched would only be a few of the games those children could play at.

The following day the dreamers watched the children going to school again and this time they went into the other class. This time the teacher was a tall bald headed man and he was wearing a long overall. He looked very strict, but not as cruel as the other teacher. The children were sitting at their desks. Two at each desk with boys on the left and girls on the right. The lesson was on arithmetic and the work was not being done on paper, but on boards of slate. The children were writing on the slates with slender pencils. The teacher was walking round the class and complimenting some on the progress they were making, when suddenly the silence was shattered by the church bells ringing furiously. The teacher told the children to stop work at once, get their belongings and run straight home.

The four dreamers also ran out to see what had happened and there were a lot of people leaving their homes and heading to the end of the village beyond the church. As the dreamers passed the church they saw a field with some small ponies in it and beyond this there were a number of buildings and large stacks of coal at a railway siding. It was now clear that this was a mining village and there was some sort of accident at the mine. Almost all the men of this village would work in the mine on a shift system. Every man not working was now racing to the pit and the women whose men were working were also running to the pit

At the pit a number of men were being assembled as a rescue squad and they headed to the lifts at the pithead to take them down the mine. They crowded into a large bucket and it was being lowered down. There were two lifts and an empty bucket was also being lowered to bring up any injured men. The four dreamers jumped into this and were soon heading down the mine. They thought they were never going to stop going down, but they finally arrived at a large cavern and the rescue team were preparing to go down the mineshaft. They were carrying a cage with a canary in it to give warning of any dangerous gasses that may be there. The canary would die if the gas level was too high. The danger of a gas explosion was very high and the miners were carrying special oil burning lamps. Torquil said, "I know about those lamps. They are called 'Davy' lamps and they were invented by Sir Humphrey Davy in 1815 and so the time of our visit to the past must be after this date. These lamps are safe to work in the presence of gas." Following the rescue men down the shaft the men were carrying spades and picks as they made their way through the black coal dust that covered the ground. It was a long way down the shaft and it was getting narrower all the time.

The Mining Rescue Team

The tunnel was prevented from caving in by wooden props supporting roof battens. The men at the front of the rescue team stopped and the problem lay ahead. The tunnel had collapsed and there was very little space. Someone was hitting the side of the tunnel and a shout of "Quiet everyone," echoed through the mine. There was complete silence in the gloom of the Davy lamps. The side of the tunnel was hammered again and then silence. "Listen," someone said, "I heard something." Silence again and then from further down the collapsed tunnel came a tapping sound. "They are still alive!" someone shouted and the leading miners made their way further over the fallen debris while others cleared the path of fallen rocks and fitted new pit props. After a few hundred yards the rescue came to a complete blockage and could go no further. To clear the tunnel by hand was going to be a very long job and the rescuers knew that the trapped men had only a limited time to live due to a lack of air and possible gas poisoning.

All sorts of ideas were put forward with plans of older pit workings looked at to see if there was an alternative way, but there was not much hope of saving the men. It was thought that about thirty men were trapped in the tunnel and many of the rescue team were relatives of them. The only hope was in cutting through the blockage and working non-stop round the clock in shifts. The men worked feverishly with picks and shovels driving their way further into the blockage. The four dreamers noticed an area cut out on the side of the shaft and from where men were leading pit ponies. They were harnessed to large trolleys and these were loaded with the fallen rubble to be removed from the area and allow new pit props to be fitted and prevent the tunnel collapsing on the rescuers. Every now and then the work would stop and a minute of silence would be held to listen for that faint tapping sound and there was always someone who would say they could hear it.

The work continued all day and night and the families of the miners whether trapped or in the rescue attempt waited anxiously at the pithead for news from below. The miners were a very loyal breed of men and in the mines it was all for one and one for all. All endured the hard work and had great respect for each other. The collapsed tunnel had been cleared for about fifty yards, but they still seemed no nearer the trapped men and it was a long time since any tapping sound had been heard. There was no let up in the ferocity the rescuers were working with one shift relieving another. A sudden cry of alarm came from the rescuers cutting through the blockage and a shout of "Flood" filled the air with dread. Water was seeping through from the blocked tunnel and the more the blockage was being cleared, the greater the water flow until soon a small stream was running through the shaft. Fears were now that the trapped miners had drowned and there was also the fear that the blocked tunnel was holding back a wall of water that could burst through and drown everyone in the mine. This was indeed a problem and the leader of the rescue team had to decide what to do. He decided to continue working until the last possible moment and called for hand pumps to be brought down and set up to pump the water away.

The leaking water was having an effect on the material blocking the tunnel and it was making it easier to clear and progress was more rapid. The stream of water was a constant flow now and the rescuers knew that their time was running out. The pumps were keeping the shaft clear as they pumped the water into an old and lower mine working. Suddenly there was a shout of terror from the rescuers digging as the force of the water surged through and material blocking the tunnel was forced on top of them. It was thought that this was the end and the rescue attempt would have to be abandoned as the men were freed from the rubble on top of them. Such was the thought of flood waters coming through that no one realised that men were trying to clamber over the debris from the other side and the trapped men had been reached.

The scenes of sheer comradeship as the rescued men embraced their rescuers was amazing, but the problems were not over yet. Some of the trapped men were injured in the tunnel collapse and it was going to be difficult to get them out. The pit road was liable to collapse and the rising waters could drown everyone. The pit doctor came down to examine the men's injuries, and do some first aid and advise on the safe way to lift the men and get them out of the pit without further injury.

The four dreamers were just in a dream as they had watched all this from the beginning and they made their way back to the lift and managed to get back to the pithead. At the pit head the news of the rescue was greeted with a loud cheering and the weeping was now of joy rather than sadness. It took all day to get all the men out of the mine and the four dreamers had a look into the houses on the miners' rows. They were usually just with two rooms. There was a coal fire for heating and cooking and paraffin lamps for lighting. One room was used as the living room, but it also had a bed recess. The other room was a bedroom.

The toilets were dry lavatories outside and the bath was a large tub that had to be filled with water heated on the fire. In spite of these troubles, poor living conditions and risk of disease the mining villagers just seemed to accept this way of life where everyone is taken as an equal.

The four dreamers were happy to see the miners saved, but they knew that in many other mines the outcome was disastrous with many lives lost. Calum said, "I will think about this trip every time I see a smoking chimney and remember those men who work with danger every minute to get that coal."

Morag said, "The day we watched those girls playing made me feel so humble and their little songs will always be in my mind."

Flora said, "I will enjoy school much more than I did before. When I think of the way those children were treated by that wicked woman. She was the opposite from the other women in that village."

Torquil said, "I don't think we will ever find out where we have been taken on this trip's visit to the past as there have been so many pit disasters, but it does not matter because we have learned a lesson on this trip and that is that we must appreciate how lucky we are. Let's go back to Strathbrochan." They unclasped their hands and the friendly mist swirled around them to soon lift and return them to Loch Brochan.

13
A Dead End Journey

There was not the usual trip to the mobile library after the trip to the coal mining village as they did not know the name of the village they had visited, or the mine disaster they had witnessed, but it was not long before the children of Strathbrochan were playing 'Leavo', trying new tricks with skipping ropes, or trying out the various ways of playing marbles. The four dreamers were so affected by the enjoyment the children in that mining village had playing their games that they were determined to introduce all the games they had seen to the children of Strathbrochan. For the time being the computer games were forgotten as the games shown to them by the dreamers were far more enjoyable and they were played at every opportunity.

The adults of Strathbrochan were amazed at the children's enjoyment playing the old games, but the biggest mystery was where did the four dreamers learn about all those games, because they had never been played before at Strathbrochan. It was no use asking any of the dreamers where they had learned the games, as the dreamers knew that they would not be believed and people would laugh at them.

The next time the four dreamers were hoping to return to Loch Brochan and see if another trip could be possible before going back to school after the holiday would be on Easter Monday. The problem was that so many things had been arranged for that day and they would have to wait until Monday and see if time would be available.

Monday came and it looked as if the trip to Loch Brochan would have to be cancelled, but as the day wore on it became clear that the four dreamers would be free to go at three o'clock and this was arranged. It was a rush to get ready and the walk to Loch Brochan was quicker than usual with the knowledge that they would have to be back early, as they had to go visiting with their parents that night. At the loch they clasped hands tightly and awaited the vapour cloud as it swirled over towards them and they were once again travelling through space.

The mist cleared and the four dreamers were on the platform of a railway station. The platform was quite busy and the people waiting for the train were all very well dressed. Some of the men were wearing bowler hats and a few had top hats and the dreamers thought that they were back in the 19th century. The name of the station was Burntisland and the children knew that this was on the Firth of Forth. Some of the passengers were talking and they were saying that the Edinburgh train was late, but at that moment a train pulled into the station. The four dreamers were quite excited and looking forward to a trip to Edinburgh and what would await them there.

The engine had a plate on it with the No. 224. The first carriage was third class and most of the passengers boarded this. The next carriage was first class and only a few people were entering it. As nobody could see the four dreamers they decided that they would travel in style and, as the door of the central compartment had been opened by someone they jumped in. Another three carriages followed the first class carriage and the remainder of the passengers occupied those. A guard's van completed the train.

A platform attendant came along slamming all the open carriage doors shut before blowing his whistle and waving a green flag. The engine driver gave a hoot on a steam horn and they were off. It was a dark night, the wind was howling and the rain was lashing down

Calum was looking puzzled. He said, "If this train is going to Edinburgh and this is early in the 1880s the Forth Rail Bridge was not built until 1890. How will this train get to Edinburgh?" This caused the others to think about the same and the name of the next station the train would stop at was awaited with interest.

It was not too long before they would find out, but they were surprised when they could make out the name of the station in the dim gaslight to be Kinghorn. None of the four knew where it was, although Torquil and Morag had heard of it, they could not remember where it was. After a short stop the train moved off again and soon it was drawing in to another bigger station, but still dimly lit and the station name was seen to be Kircaldy. This puzzled the dreamers even more as they knew Kircaldy was in Fife and in the opposite direction from where they thought the train would be going. Where on earth was this trip into the past going to lead them. All they could do was sit and wait. The carriage was comfortable with padded armrests and as they had to keep their hands clasped they could rest their arms.

The stations on the route were noted and they were such as Dysart, Thornton Junction, Markinch, Falkland, Kingskettle, Ladybank Junction. At Ladybank Junction a number of people joined the train and they could hear people on the platform saying that they had come from Perth. Luckily no one came into their compartment. The dreamers started guessing as to where they would end up and the favourite place was St Andrews, as they knew that there was a lot of history connected with that town. It was very dark outside and the wind and rain were pounding the train as it battled through what was now a gale. The names of a couple of stations were missed and it was a long time before they stopped at a station called Leuchars. The station clock was at seven o'clock. "I know where Leuchars is," said Torquil. "There is an RAF station there. I wonder if we should have got off the train here or someplace along the route, or have we just to wait until the train stops at its terminus, wherever that may be. It is certainly not Edinburgh."

The train chuffed out of the station into the storm and as it thundered on its way the four dreamers just relaxed and wondered where they were going. Morag said, "I think we must be going to Dundee as that is the next big city going north. Surely we are not going to Aberdeen." The train stopped at another small station and no name could be seen. This was a very short stop and the train was soon driving through the gale and it was taking a right buffeting from the wind making it sway slightly from side to side. The four dreamers were sitting in silence and suddenly they felt the train was going faster. Torquil said; "It feels as if we are flying." He had hardly time to finish saying this before the front of the carriage dropped and the compartment they were in split in two and the seat they were sitting on was hurled out into the darkness and the storm before they plunged under water still clinging to the arms of the seat. The seat came to the surface and was being tossed about in the wild waves before it crashed into and got wedged in steelwork sticking out of a stone pillar.

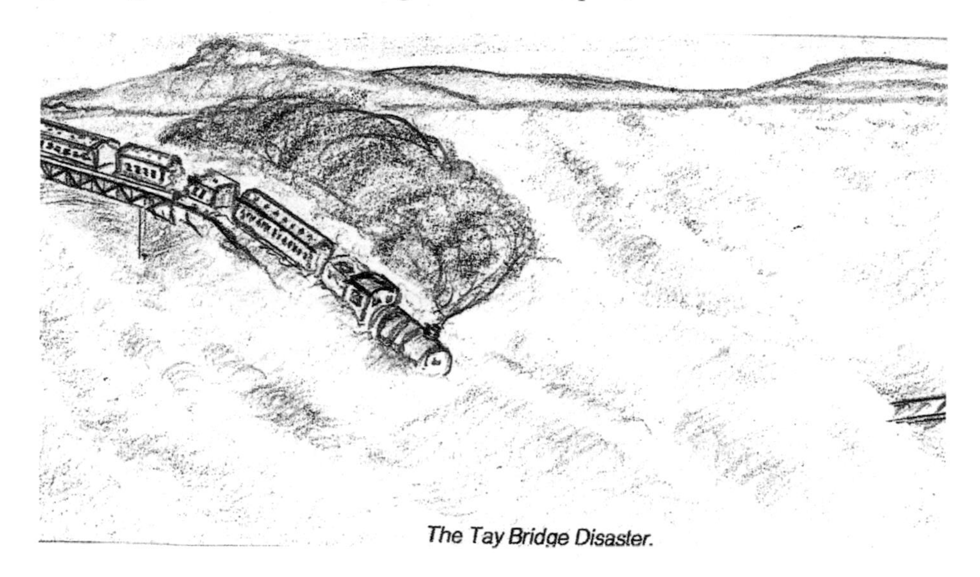

The Tay Bridge Disaster.

The four dreamers knew that they could have broken their clasped hands and returned safely to Loch Brochan, but they had to see what was happening. This after all was their visit to the past and they wanted to see and experience this event. They knew that they were just as ghosts and would not be harmed.

Still clinging to the wedged seat they looked all around them in the darkness and the only sound was of the crashing waves and the howling wind. As their eyes became accustomed to the darkness they could make out the structure of a bridge that stopped suddenly. The stone pillar the seat had collided with was the remains of the support the next section of the bridge had rested on, but it was now gone and so also was the rest of the bridge as far as they could see.

The No 224 train they had come to know as the Edinburgh train had raced onto the bridge unaware that the storm had destroyed the centre section of the bridge and plunged off into the wild waters of the Firth of Tay dragging the rest of the train with it.

The four dreamers thought about all the people on that train and with the experience they had come through they knew that it was all over in seconds. The people on that train would never have known what was happening to them. Some of them would probably have been sleeping. The sudden increase of speed would not have been noticed until the carriage plunged into the waters and they would all have been killed instantly. By the time they could have realised that anything was wrong they would be dead. It is unlikely they would have suffered any pain.

As the children grew more used to the dark, faint lights could be seen far away on the shore and it was obvious that this had been a very long bridge and they now knew they had witnessed the disaster of the Tay Rail Bridge and Morag was right in thinking that the train was bound for Dundee, but that was not the destination for this journey into the past. Somehow the quickness of this tragedy prevented a feeling of terror, or the gruesome scenes they had seen at Culloden. They now lay there clutching that carriage seat and they knew that when the disaster was discovered a search would be made for survivors.

It was a long time before there was any feeling of anxiety by the staff, or people waiting for relatives at Dundee because the train had been on time at Leuchars and that any delay would be due to the storm. The worrying began when half an hour after the train was due there was no sign of it and questions were being asked. It was known that the train had stopped once after leaving Leuchars and fears of a fault at the bridge due to the weather were being checked out. It was found that the train had gone on to the bridge on time and the failure of it to arrive at the other end brought the full impact of the disaster to light when the centre section of the bridge was gone and the train with it.

It was hours before the four dreamers heard shouting and a boat was approaching to look for survivors. They were checking everything anyone surviving could be clinging to and the bridge pillars sticking out of the water were being searched. The boat finally came to the pillar the dreamers were on and when the men saw the seat their hopes were raised that someone could be saved, but of course they could not see the children, who as soon as the boat was pulled alongside they managed to keep together and jump aboard. The men on the boat were policemen and they continued their difficult task in those stormy waters until they were sure that no one had survived.

They returned to the distant shore and followed by the dreamers they went to tell the people waiting for news about the disaster. It was at that moment the dreamers felt the full impact of this tragedy as they saw the grief and sorrow and the thought of what the relatives of the people on that train would suffer. Probably for the rest of their lives.

Calum said, “This is the second time we have seen a disaster. The last one in the coal mine where the miners were rescued and now this disaster where all life has been lost. It just shows that we never know what can happen.”

Morag said, “The people who had their lives cut short on that bridge would never know what happened, but I will always feel sorrow for the families of these people. They will all be asking the question why did this happen?”

Torquil said, “We must look on every day as a gift and make the best of the time we have, because we could be the people on a train, or in some other circumstance just like the tragedy of the 224.”

Flora said, “I think of the train driver, fireman and guard. They left their homes just to do their job never thinking that they would never return. This has been a very sad trip and I think we should get back to Strathbrochan.” They unclasped their hands and when the mist cleared they were glad to be back on the shore of Loch Brochan..

This trip into the past was covered in quick time and the children were back in Strathbrochan by 4.30pm. Although this was the last day of the Easter holiday weekend they were all keen to get back to school the next day with the anticipation of a visit to the mobile library to search for the story of the Tay Bridge Disaster.

The mobile library had also been on holiday and so it came on Tuesday.

Mrs McNab, the librarian, saw the four dreamers coming towards the van and she wondered what book would be in demand this time and she was surprised to hear them ask for information on the Tay Bridge Disaster. Mrs McNab hunted for some time before being able to locate such a book and the details in the book were quickly read by the children and it brought the whole disaster back vividly to their minds.

The train No 224 was the connection for people coming from Edinburgh and travelling on to Dundee. This was why it was called the Edinburgh train and it had left Burntisland station at 4.43pm. The Tay Bridge had only been completed 19 months earlier and was designed by Thomas Bouch. The reason for the bridge collapse was not solely due to the violent storm, but also to bad design and faulty workmanship. A new Tay Rail Bridge was constructed and opened eight years and four months later by Sir William Arrol the famous Scottish builder of bridges throughout the world. At the time of building it was the longest rail bridge in the world at 10,780 feet (two miles 211feet).

It was with sorrow they read that 75 people perished that fateful Sunday night on 28 December 1879. It would have been a very sad New Year for the relatives and friends of these people and there were tears in the eyes of one of the dreamers as she thought of that night and the recovery of only four bodies from the sea.

It was surprising to read that the engine No 224 was salvaged from the depths and restored to working order to run for many years after the disaster including trips over the new bridge. The four dreamers could imagine this as a ghost train with the spirits of the people who perished completing the journey they had started on the road to Dundee after all those years.

14
The Wild Side of Strathbrochan

Months had now passed since the excitement of the four dreamers' adventures in the snow, but there was still an interest by the media in the village of Strathbrochan.

Colonel Maxwell was approached to allow a television company to film his estate and requested the services of John Hunter his gamekeeper, as his expertise would be required. Colonel Maxwell and Lady Maxwell were thrilled at the thought of having their estate being on television and willingly gave John Hunter permission to work with the television people. Colonel Maxwell said, "Since the interest in the village of Strathbrochan had been due to the four children rescued from the snow, I think that they should be included in the filming by the TV Company."

This was readily agreed and arrangements were made with the children's parents. It was decided to allow the children three days absence from school during the filming.

When the four dreamers heard this they were really excited at the thought of being on television and taking part in a wildlife film of the area.

There were no wild animals as such, but there were deer, rabbits, hares, foxes, badgers, otters, pheasants, eagles, buzzards, owls, sparrow hawks plus many small creatures and birds. Although all these animals and birds lived around the area of Strathbrochan there were many villagers who had never seen some of them, like the badgers, otters and eagles and only the likes of John Hunter knew where they might be seen.

John Hunter had a meeting with the crew who would be carrying out the filming. The producer was Norman Ogilvie, the cameraman was Eric Bates and the narrator was Malcolm White. John Hunter told the crew that animals can sense the presence of humans from a long way off and they do this by scent, sound or the actions of other creatures such as birds. They can also warn each other of danger. For this reason they must travel silently and be prepared to lie in wait for long periods in the hope that an animal might appear. The direction of the wind will be a major factor in their approach to a possible place, which may be the habitat of a particular animal, because their scent will be carried for a long distance in the wind.

They would be operating in rough country where there will be peat hags and bogs to cross. Some sections will require some rock climbing and although not dangerous the hills are quite steep and strenuous to climb. Now the children coming with us will be cared for and people will be wondering if it will be alright for children to cross this rough country, well in his experience when taking children with adults, the children are sometimes more capable than the adults. Each person will require stout waterproof footwear, clothing, food, hot and cold drinks. Some of the trips will be at night and some very early in the morning.

This 'Scottish Safari' was arranged for the 1 May. All the preparations were swiftly made and there were a lot of jealous children in Strathbrochan as they watched the four dreamers set off in another adventure.

The television crew had all their equipment on a four-wheel drive vehicle and John Hunter had his Land Rover. The children would be travelling with John Hunter and he would look after them. First of all he checked that they were all suitably dressed and had enough to eat and drink with them. They had plenty to eat and drink because their mothers had made sure of that and John had actually to get them to leave some stuff in the Land Rover as they had too much to carry in their backpacks

The party moved off from the village and most of the villagers had turned out to see them off, even although it was only six o'clock in the morning. John told the children that today they would be driving along the rough tracks beyond Loch Brochan and round behind Craig Hill.

The mention of Craig Hill brought back the day of the blizzard to the four dreamers and when they got lost in the snow. It looked so safe now on this sunny morning. John said, "This track ends soon and we will have to start walking. We will then be climbing over Ben Creachan to reach Glen Morvin. Today I hope we will see some deer.

The rough track stopped at a burn and the party prepared to climb Ben Creachan. They started crossing the burn on stepping stones before the climb up the steep grassy slopes to reach some rocks and boulders, where John Hunter led the way up, always checking the children were alright, but there was no problem there as the four dreamers were thoroughly enjoying this. A few hundred feet higher up and the huffing and puffing was getting louder. A few minutes rest was taken to have a drink and a short rest. Every now and then the children thought they had reached the top only to find another summit ahead. John called these lower summits false summits and said, "It is always the same when climbing, but you come to expect it and carry on knowing that you must reach the true top sometime."

As they approached the summit John Said, "We will not go right to the summit, but cross over the ridge lower down. We will have to keep low and hide our approach as there may be deer in Glen Morven. If they see us silhouetted against the skyline they will be off and we will have travelled all this way for nothing."

The party crept up to the crest and continued until they could see down into the glen. John Hunter had checked the wind direction and it was blowing from the glen. This would prevent their scent being picked up by any animals in the glen. John was leading and he suddenly held up his arm and whispered, "Quiet, come and look."

As the party reached John and looked further down into the glen an amazing sight was below. There were hundreds of deer gathered in the glen feeding on the grasses and small shrubbery. The TV cameras were set up with telephoto lens and they started to film from what was a very long way from the deer.

John said, "See that gully over to the left we should be able to make our way down and at the bottom there is a lot of cover and we will be able to get very close to the herd." It was rough going clambering down the gully, where the splashing of a small stream hid any noise they made. It was worth the struggle as they came out slightly above the herd and about fifty yards from it. The cameraman Eric Bates was soon filming excitedly and occasionally a stag with its huge antlers would strut around a group of hinds to make sure his family were protected. Later this movement of the stags became more rapid and John said, "They are about to move to new pastures." And sure enough the whole herd started to run down the glen. Every now and then the stags would stop to check all their family were following and the pace increased until the whole herd vanished out of sight. The TV crew were really happy. They had obtained some wonderful close up photographs and the galloping off made a great end to the deer filming.

It was now time to have a well-earned lunch and the four dreamers enjoyed the food their mothers had packed for them. The departure of the deer did not, however, stop filming, as the scenery was breathtaking. It was too early to see the hills in bloom with the purple heather, but the fresh green grasses were an excellent substitute. An occasional sparrow hawk hovering over its unsuspecting prey also added to the variety of the day's filming.

Time to head for home now and there was no need for stealth so they did not have to climb up the gully, but took to the grassy slopes to reach the crest of Ben Creachan. At the top John mentioned to the others to take care on the way down as this was when knees took a pounding and accidents could easily happen due to tiredness at the end of the day.

The descent was made with no complaints and the group headed back to Strathbrochan and the full impact of the day's climb was felt as they stepped out of the cars. The aches in their legs were more than they expected and the children were glad to get home, have a hot bath and an early night in their beds.

The following day did not have an early start as John Hunter intended to try and take the TV crew to film some badgers. This was an animal that few people in Strathbrochan had seen. The plan was to leave Strathbrochan at two o'clock in the afternoon to arrive at the location where John expected the badgers could be filmed before it was too dark, but special photographic equipment would be required if darkness came down early.

It was expected to get dark around 7.30pm

This was not going to be such a strenuous day as yesterday, but refreshments were carried. The route taken was through Colonel Maxwell's Estate on rough tracks through the dense pine forest to reach a very remote area where few people ever visited. Leaving the forest the route was over rough grassland to reach an old deciduous forest covering some small hills. John Hunter stopped the vehicles at the edge of the forest and led the group into the forest to a hollow on the side of the hill. The time was only 5.30pm and John said, "Let's settle down comfortably in this hollow and keep as quiet as possible." He said to the four dreamers, "Just imagine you are ghosts and make no sound." He failed to notice the smile that appeared on the children's faces. They decided to have a meal while they waited for the light to fade.

Some Of Strathbrochans Wildlife.

When darkness began to fall, John got the TV crew to crawl up to the top of the hollow and look over to rising ground beyond a ditch. A hole between two large boulders could be seen at the bottom of this rise and John got the crew to focus their cameras on this area. He urged everyone to keep completely silent. It was not too dark as there was a half moon giving some light through the trees. It was all the dreamers could do not to speak and it seemed an eternity before John motioned his arm towards the hole on the opposite embankment. Something was moving and the TV crew started their cameras with the infra-red equipment all connected. There was a slight whirr from the camera, but the animal was still at the entrance to what must have been its sett. Slowly it emerged with its pointed snout sniffing the air until the full body of an adult badger appeared with the black and white stripes on its head quite visible in the poor light. Another badger came slowly behind the first and they were extremely cautious animals. It was obvious that the slightest sound or scent would send them scurrying back down into their den. However, the favourable wind direction and the silence of the group prevented their detection. The two adult badgers were pushing their snouts into the loose earth and grass at the sett entrance looking for insects and they were followed by two smaller badgers. As they emerged they started to roll each other over. This was a wonderful sight and a treat to watch. This would be the highlight of today's filming. The badger family started to walk along the ditch and John waited until they were well out of sight before he signalled to the group to move silently away from the area.

The four dreamers thought how great it was to experience this sight of such rare animals so near to Strathbrochan and they could see that John Hunter wanted to keep it that way.

The return to Strathbrochan was uneventful and the children were advised to get to bed early as the start of tomorrow's 'Safari' was to be at 7am. The excitement of the children at dinner that night bubbled out as they told their parents of seeing the badgers. None of their parents had ever seen them and the children had been told by John Hunter never to tell anyone where the badger sett was.

The third day was to be the last of filming and the aim today was to film some otters and they were another animal that few people in Strathbrochan knew about. It was also hoped to see an eagle, as the area they were going to was quite mountainous.

The four dreamers were up early and they made sure their backpacks were filled with what they would require for what was going to be a long day in a mountainous area.

At 7 o'clock the party set off and headed round the other side of Creag Hill, but this time there was no track and the four-wheel drives were essential to cross the open countryside. On the way they disturbed dozens of rabbits and on one occasion saw a fox skulking away. It was some time after passing Creag Hill when Torquil gave a shout and pointed away to the left, "Look," he shouted, "there is that old hut that gave us shelter from the storm." And the other dreamers remembered that time in the snow. No wonder it had been so hard to find them as they were now a long way from Strathbrochan. When the film crew heard that, that was the hut the children had been rescued from they asked John to go over to it although it was a good distance out of their way. They thought this would be good for their film and photographed the children standing beside the hut.

Onward now and passing a cliff face where a small river seemed to be flowing from under the cliff. There were some gorse bushes growing along the bank and as he looked, Calum thought he saw a man jumping behind the bushes. He thought the man looked familiar and he looked like Archie Reid, but surely this was too far from Strathbrochan for Archie to be poaching. Calum never mentioned this to John Hunter because he knew that they tried to outdo each other.

Leaving the cliff they travelled through a glen and John said, "We will leave the vehicles here and continue on foot. Keep as quiet as you can." They walked for about half a mile to reach a small lochan with a burn running out of it at the far end. There were plenty of gorse bushes to give cover and John checked the wind direction to see if it was carrying their scent ahead of them, but it was favourable.

John told the film crew to creep along behind the gorse bushes out of sight of the lochan to where the burn flowed out at the far end and to set up their cameras to focus around that area. John said, "We will just have to wait now and hope an otter appears, but we must be extremely quiet because otters can hear sounds from a great distance.

From this favourable position they had a clear view of the area that John had pointed out to them. There were no signs of any movement on the water and they decided that this was a good time for a meal while they waited. They kept very quiet as they ate and watched the water for any sign of movement. They finished their meal and sat there quietly for another two hours. John whispered, "I think we are going to be disappointed. The otters seem to be elsewhere today. We will wait another ten minutes and then leave." He had hardly finished this when Flora whispered, "There is something in the water down there." And she pointed further along the lochan from where the cameras were focussed.

John looked in the direction of her finger and said, "It is the otters." Six otters were emerging from close to the bank and they started to frolic about in the water and one of the larger otters appeared with a fish in its mouth. They slowly splashed and played their way along the lochan and went right into the area the cameras were sighted on. The telescopic lenses brought the otters right into focus and wonderful pictures were obtained of these otters in their natural environment. This was a very successful day.

Satisfied with the filming the party quietly withdrew and drove back to go up a glen behind the cliff they had seen on the way and it led to the other side of the cliff. John Hunter said, "There used to be an eagle's nest or eyrie near here and if we climb up this hill and look over the cliff we should be able to look down into it. There was no sign of any eagles flying in the sky above the cliff as they started to climb up the steep grassy slope and it was not long before the flat grassy top of the cliff was reached and John asked the TV crew to get the cameras ready. He also warned the four dreamers to keep back from the edge of the cliff. John walked over to the edge and slowly walked round the cliff top. He had not gone far when suddenly there was a loud flapping sound and an eagle soared up from the side of the cliff just ahead of him. He got quite a fright and thought that the eagle might attack him, but it flew high above and glided in a circular flight around the cliff. The TV crew were glad John had warned them to be ready and the eagle was soon in focus. John Hunter lay flat on his stomach and peered over the cliff edge and he found himself looking straight down into the eyrie and there was another eagle sitting in the nest that John said was the female. The four dreamers were allowed to lie beside John and they looked down to see a sight that few people had ever seen and the cameraman also crept forward and photographed the eagle in the eyrie. The eagle above was still circling and John said, "Let's not stay any longer because if that eagle thinks we are going to touch the eyrie he will attack us and one of us could be seriously injured." They started to collect all the equipment and then headed back along the flat top with John Hunter leading, the TV crew next and the four dreamers behind. Flora was last and walking a little to the right of the others looking sky-wards to watch for the eagle. There was a terrified scream and when everyone turned round Flora had gone; completely disappeared. Rushing to where she was last seen there was a hole in the ground hidden by the grass and it was down here that Flora had fallen. Torquil shouted frantically, "Flora! Flora!" but there was no reply. John Hunter peered down the hole and he thought that Flora was gone forever. He had his mobile phone and immediately called the police. He gave them their position and asked for immediate assistance form every available source. Especially the helicopter rescue and medical team. Peering down the hole there was darkness and the only sound was of running water far below. The hole was not big enough for a man to go down and Flora must just have been small enough to slide down. The ground around the top of the hole was soft and looked as if it could fall into the hole and they had to stand back for fear of knocking the soft earth into the hole. They just stood there feeling absolutely useless to help Flora. John Hunter was shattered to think he had lost a young girl in his care and he was worrying about Flora's parents when they would hear about this tragedy. This was something he could never have imagined to happen. He had seen small holes in the hills before, but never more than a few feet deep. The three dreamers were crying and the TV crew were feeling responsible for bringing these children out on the hills just because they wanted a film.

Thirty minutes passed and the helicopter arrived with ropes and lifting gear, but no matter what they tried to do there was no answer as to how they were going to get down that hole to save Flora. The only way to get down was to bring in excavation equipment to cut a wider hole, but if Flora was lying unconscious falling stones could kill her. It would also be very difficult to widen the hole because there was only a foot of soft earth and then it was solid rock. Floras name was repeatedly shouted, but there was no response.

Another hour passed and a constant stream of assistance arrived. The mountain rescue team; Doctor Nichols and Nurse Simpson. The police and of course the media as news was spreading fast. There must have been about thirty people on that cliff top and by that time the eagle was long gone. There was not one person on that cliff top with any idea as each suggestion proved to be impractical. Silence fell over the scene as everyone thought of little Flora and how helpless they were. Morag stopped sobbing and shouted, "Listen!" There was silence again as they listened as the top of the hole. "No not there," shouted Morag, "From the bottom of the cliff."

Then came the distant voice of Flora shouting, "I'm alright!" There was a stampede down from that cliff top and there sitting on the bank of the burn coming out of the bottom of the cliff was Flora with a huge grin on her face. She had fallen right down the hole through the cliff into a small pool and floated through a passage in the rock and finally outside into the open air. This was a miracle. There were no tears of sorrow now, just thankfulness and John Hunter rushed over and hugged Flora as she lay there covered in mud and soaking wet, but she was happy to be back with the dreamers. Doctor Nichols examined her and had her wrapped up in warm blankets and the entire rescue force made their way back to Strathbrochan.

This was Strathbrochan in the news again and again with a happy ending. Flora's parents could not believe their daughter could be the centre of such excitement, but the only thing they were interested in was that she was back home safe and well.

The television filming was a complete success and the addition of the hut the dreamers had been saved from, the perfect filming of the areas wildlife and of course the dramatic climax to the project made one of the greatest documentary films produced by the TV company. Malcolm White, the narrator of the film, almost ran out of adjectives when describing some of the scenes.

When the four dreamers met again Flora told them when she suddenly fell down that hole in the ground she landed in a pool of water and she slowly had made her way down what was like a water chute and she could see daylight at the bottom, but her backpack kept getting stuck on rocks and it took a long time to get it free. When she reached the place where the burn came out of the cliff she said she got really stuck and she thought she was going to faint, but she said that she got the feeling that somebody outside was pulling her free and the next thing she knew she was lying on the river bank and she thought she was all alone, until she heard the sounds from the cliff top and shouted I'm alright.

Calum listened to Flora's story and the part that interested him was when she said that she felt as if someone was pulling her free. Was this the man he had seen when they first saw the burn coming out of the cliff and was that man Archie Reid? Was Archie the man who had finally saved Flora?

Flora's route through the mountain

15
The Beginning

From being a quiet and relatively unknown village, Strathbrochan was now one of the best-known villages in Scotland and this was all due to the four dreamers of Strathbrochan.

An air of excitement hung over the village throughout April as many visitors were attracted to the village after seeing the TV film and the four dreamers were always at the centre of things.

There was a holiday on the first of May and this date was chosen by the dreamers to make another trip to Loch Brochan. They headed for the loch and a new adventure. The usual clasping of hands brought the swirling vapours over them and they were travelling through time once again.

This time the mist remained around them for a very long time and when it finally lifted the children could see nothing at all because all around them was total darkness. Not even the twinkling of a star and then they realised that they were not standing on solid ground, but suspended in space. There was not a word spoken by the children and they feared what was going to happen next.

A glow appeared high above them and this glow gradually became brighter and brighter until it was like a flaming ball of fire and above it a blue haze formed and then turned to clear blue. As the children looked at this the fear they had felt when the mist lifted was now replaced by a calm peaceful presence and Morag said, “Is that not the most beautiful sky you have ever seen?”

“Yes,” said Torquil, “and look at that little bright light shining high above us it reminds me of that light we saw when the comet crashed into Loch Brochan. I wonder if that is the comet being created."

All this time they had been looking up, but the light now revealed what lay below as they hung in space. Below was a dense dark mist and as they watched it became lighter and less dense to reveal a vast ocean with only water visible in all directions and looking like a great ball of water. The light from the sun above faded as it dropped below the watery horizon and once again the four dreamers were in total darkness.

The glow re-appeared from the opposite horizon and again the beautiful sky and the waters were illuminated and there was a distinct separation between the waters below and the sky above. As the children watched they were amazed to see huge spouts of water rising from the seas and those waterspouts changed to roaring pillars of fire. It was like a gigantic fireworks display. The pillars originally of water were now fountains of molten rock and as they raged the rock became solid in the ocean and large areas of the ocean were now covered with rock and the scene below now changed to look more like the planet earth as the four dreamers knew it with land and sea.

The sea was pounding the rocky shores and the red-hot rock was being ground into sand, which was also being blown by the wind over the rocks and forming fields of sand over large areas. The seas calmed and the wind died down to leave below what the dreamers now knew for sure to be planet earth. They also knew that the great ball of fire now disappearing below the horizon was the sun and total darkness returned as it dropped out of sight.

Again the dreamers were waiting for the sunrise and the scene below was changing again. Gone was the black and grey to be replaced with the greens of grasses on the sandy fields. As they watched other colours appeared as more plants were being fed by some magic fertilizer and it was forcing their growth from seeds to seedling in one complete cycle. There were many types of trees now and they were producing fruit. As the sun was setting the seed falling from the plants was again starting to sprout and the world was being clad with greenery in all the arable land that appeared.

The setting of the sun brought the darkness again, but as the four dreamers watched pinpoints of light appeared in the dark sky and slowly they became brighter and sparkled as they gradually produced a glimmer of light on earth. Some were solitary lights in the dark background, some in little groups and others in groups of many thousand all twinkling in the sky.

From amidst the stars another solitary light appeared and it grew in size and the dreamers knew that this was the moon and the earth now had light at night and the sun in the day giving light and heat. As the earth below was now revolving, day, night, summer, autumn, winter and spring were being created on earth and the four dreamers all had their own thoughts on how this was happening. They had now seen the creation of the sun, moon and stars. They had also seen the earth being made, not as they know it now, but as it was formed in the beginning.

The sun arose in the morning and all below was peaceful. The four dreamers were aware that they were slowly descending until their feet landed on the grass. There was a gentle slope leading down to a sandy beach. The children walked down to the water's edge and watched the waves rippling in. Suddenly there was a splash and then another and fish were leaping out of the water.

Calum said, "I think we are now seeing the start of life on earth." They searched in some small sandy pools and they could see little creatures like crabs and shrimps moving about in the sandy bottom of the pools. As the day progressed more and more signs of life were seen and the four dreamers were really excited when a spout of water drew their attention to a little white whale further out in the bay. In the morning all things living on earth seemed to be in the water, but later the jumping of small fish seemed to attract some birds that just seemed to come out of the air. They were all white with yellow beaks and red feet. They had appeared like little ghosts. As daylight faded the moon appeared and the quiet of the night was broken only by the rippling waves as they melted into the sandy shore.

The sun was bright in the sky the next morning and the four dreamers walked away from the shore and through some shrubbery. There was a rustling in the long grasses and the dreamers started to look for the cause of this and as they came to a clearing some animals were walking about. They were all white, some the size of rabbits, while others were more goat or sheep like and others could be described as cattle, but none of them were like any animal they had ever seen. They moved about slowly with a sort of ghostly movement as if they were just newly born and not quite sure what to do or where they were. The four dreamers knew that this was the start of life on earth.

Darkness fell and the four dreamers were looking forward to the following day. Torquil said, “We have seen the creation of the heavens, the earth, the plant and animal life. Tomorrow we may see the creation of man.” They walked back through the shrubbery in the moonlight to return to the grassy spot where they had first put their feet on earth, but Flora tripped and as she fell the linked hands parted and the chain was broken. They were soon covered with the mist and hurtling forward through time to once again return to the shore of Loch Brochan, with the sun shining brightly on the still waters.

The four dreamers stood in silence unable to move or speak as the miracle they had witnessed took over their thoughts. Morag was the first to speak, “I wish people in Strathbrochan would believe us if we told them about this trip back to the creation of the world. It would be wonderful.”

Flora said, “I’m sorry I tripped and broke the clasped hands, but I did not trip deliberately. If I had not tripped we may have seen the first man on earth. Maybe the trip was meant to happen and we were not to be allowed to see God’s final creation.”

They headed for home with their own thoughts, not of Strathbrochan, but of the wonders they had been privileged to see and the astonishing thing about all this is that the whole witnessing of the world’s creation had been seen in two and a half hours.

The beginning

16
A Strange Encounter

The four dreamers were very quiet during the following week as their thoughts were always occupied with what they had seen from a position in space and then to have stepped onto the earth at the beginning of time. It was another two weeks before the urge to go back to Loch Brochan returned as there was a feeling of what more could they possibly see of bygone times. They knew that they would never again witness the wonders they had seen on the previous visit to the past and they could not go back any further than that.

It was a Sunday afternoon and another lovely day as the four passed Mr Smith's farm on the way to Loch Brochan. They did not see Mr Smith scratch his head and mutter to himself, "There they go again. I wonder what weird tales they will be telling tomorrow?" It was second nature now just to walk to the loch, clasp hands and await the friendly mist from the loch to take them on another trip into the past. The mist appeared and off they soared to where? The fear of landing in the middle of some terrible battle was always in their minds, as the horror of Culloden was never forgotten.

This time the journey through time was quite short and when the mist cleared they found themselves on a harbour wall and they wondered where this could be. Torquil said, "I think I have been here before, but I can't remember the name, although it is quite different to when I was here. My father and mother were on holiday in the west of Scotland and we visited small fishing villages like this, but they were more modern than this place."

There were a number of fishing boats in the harbour, but the tide was out and some of the boats were lying to one side, as the water was too shallow for them to float. There were no people about and darkness was falling. Sounds of voices were coming from a building in the village and the four dreamers walked up to find an inn with a number of men drinking at a bar. It was a really old place and it did not look very clean. By the style of their dress the men all seemed to be fishermen.

The four dreamers walked up through the village and it was very quiet. The houses looked as if the people were very poor and the lights in the houses seemed to be from paraffin lamps. Walking back to the inn the dreamers were thinking what can this place be famous for and why have we been brought back to this little village? Most of the men had left leaving only two fishermen. They were raising their voices and the argument became so serious that one man struck the other and a fight developed. One man was quite old and the other was a younger man with a beard and he was quite tall. He was wearing a cloth cap and what looked like a captain's uniform and he had long boots on his feet. The fight seemed to be over money and the younger man was too strong and he was on top, but the older man managed to grasp what looked like a long wooden club and strike his opponent on the head. The young man rolled over and lay motionless.

"He has killed him!" yelled Morag, and sure enough the man was dead. They had just witnessed a murder and could do nothing about it. The older man looked worried for he had not intended to kill this man and had struck him in panic.

The older man wrapped the body in a large blanket and pulled the body outside. He went behind the inn and came back with a wheelbarrow. He loaded his victim on to it and wheeled it down to the harbour. Looking all around to make sure no one was watching he headed for a small fishing boat. He hauled the body on to it and pulled it down into a cabin where there was a large crate. He pushed the body into this and locked it. It was obvious that this man owned this boat and intended dumping the body out at sea.

Torquil said, "Why have we been shown this? It does not seem to have anything to do with a historical event. We do not even know the names of these people, or the year we have been brought back to. It must be a long time ago because there are no motor cars about and the fishing boats have sails."

After hiding the body the man went back to a house in the village and he stayed there all night. The following morning as dawn was breaking a number of men appeared at the harbour and the man who had killed the man the previous night came to meet them. There was a high wind blowing and the sea was very rough.

"Will you be risking the fishing the day Captain?" somebody shouted, and a man approached.

"That we will," said the Captain. "Get aboard and get the tackle ready. This auld boat can sail in any weather."

Four men jumped on board and started to work on the nets and getting supplies ready. "Where is Tom?" shouted one man.

"He's not feeling well," said the Captain. The ship was ready to sail in about half an hour and it set sail for the harbour entrance. Some other men had gathered to watch them sail and one of them was heard saying, "Captain Watson's a brave man to set sail wi' a sea like that. A widnie dae it for a' the fish in the sea."

The little boat sailed out of the harbour and the children watched it bobbing about on the high waves. One time it was on top of a wave and then it would plunge down into a trough before riding the next wave.

The four dreamers knew that it was not really to fish that Captain Watson had set sail, but to get rid of the body he had stowed in that trunk he had in his cabin. The small boat was soon out of sight and the four dreamers were at a loss as to what would happen next as this was a very quiet little village. Some people were working, taking fish out of a strange looking building and loading them on to a lorry pulled by a horse. When they got closer the four dreamers could see inside this building and it was full of ice.

"This is an ice house," said Calum. "I've read about them and they were used before refrigeration was invented. The ice would keep for long periods in these houses and was stored in the winter months. The fish must be distributed locally in this way."

The children remained in the village all day and there was not much activity except for a few people chatting in small groups. Night came and the dreamers decided that they had still to find out why they had been brought to this village. They went back to the inn and sat on a long bench to pass the night.

In the early morning they heard a commotion outside and when they went out there were women sobbing at the harbour and some men were getting into small boats and going out to sea. The sea was calmer now, but the children heard the people saying that the 'Sea Rose' should have been back hours ago and there was no sign of it. The villagers waited at the harbour until midday and the small boats that had left earlier were returning. "The Sea Rose is gone," someone shouted from a returning small boat and he held up a board with the name 'Sea Rose' on it. This was the only part of the boat that had sailed off into the storm that remained. No survivors were found and the village was in mourning.

Thinking that this was the reason for their visit to the past to witness the dangers that fishermen faced every time they went to sea made them feel admiration for these brave men, but it still seemed a mystery as to why they had to see a murder first before the tragedy at sea. "Let's go back to Strathbrochan," said Morag and they were just about to unclasp their hands when the mist swirled around them and they were being taken through time and space to another place.

When the mist cleared they were on a lonely track leading away from a few houses and a signpost indicated the path to Sandwood Bay. The dreamers started to walk to Sandwood Bay and it was a lovely walk through rough country and they thought they would never come to the bay as it was a very long walk. They finally saw the sea some distance ahead and soon arrived on to a beautiful beach. To the left there were cliffs and sticking out of the water was a stone pillar just like the ones they had seen the Druid Priests use at Callanish in the Orkneys. The children wondered if they were going to see something similar being built, but there was no sign of any activity. To the right the sandy beach swept round the bay, where some large rocks looked like a small island. Walking over some rocks the four dreamers walked along the sand to the left and a figure could be seen approaching from that direction. As the figure came closer they could see that the man was dressed like a sailor. He was a tall man with a beard, wearing a uniform and a cloth cap with a skip.

Sand Wood Bay

On his feet were large, long legged boots. As he approached the children he said, "Good afternoon children."

The children replied, "Good afternoon." And the man walked on past.

The children walked on and Calum whispered, "That man is the man we saw being murdered at the inn in that small village."

Torquil said, "You are right I thought that too, but it seemed so silly to think that."

They all turned round to look after the man, but there was no one there. How could anyone disappear on such a lonely stretch of sandy beach? It was Flora who noticed that there were no footprints in the soft sand. They stood there in silence and the full meaning of their visit to the past was soon to be found.

Torquil said, "This is the first time anyone has spoken to us on any of our trips into the past."

"He must have been able to see us," said Calum. "We have seen that there were no footprints in the sand. What we have seen is the ghost of that man we saw being murdered and he is probably returning to that small village."

"I am afraid," said Flora. "Let's get back to Loch Brochan." And they quickly unclasped their hands and they were all glad when the welcome mist returned them to the shore of Loch Brochan.

They ran all the way back to Strathbrochan and as they thought about this trip a shiver would run down their backs, because this was the first time any of them had ever seen a real ghost.

17
City of Ghosts

It was surprising the effect of seeing a real ghost had on the four dreamers, but the urge to return to Loch Brochan was still as strong as ever. The only one to be a bit scared was Flora, but she knew that the others could not contact the power in the loch without her and she agreed to go on the next possible trip.

The next possible time to go back to the loch was a week on Saturday and there were a few sleepless nights for some of the dreamers as their dreams became so real due to them thinking what may lie ahead.

The Saturday date arrived and the dreamers were strangely quiet as they walked to Loch Brochan. The hands were clasped cautiously as they thought what might lie in wait for them. The hands clasped and it was too late for any of them to change their minds and they were whirled away in the vapour cloud back in time. To where?

The mist lifted and it was a very dull day, but when the children saw that they were at the entrance to Edinburgh Castle it brightened them up because they had all visited the castle at some time with their parents. This time it was rather different as they saw the guards on sentry duty clad in strange fancy uniforms and armed to the teeth with old-fashioned firearms. They felt great as they wandered past the guards and entered the castle. This was a new playground for the dreamers as they defended the castle by firing the great cannons at the enemy below. They went down to the dungeons and even looking at them filled them with horror and as they heard the groans of a prisoner locked up in one of them they rushed back out to walk the battlements and climb to the point where they had seen the lone piper play when their parents had taken them to see the military tattoo. It was great to wander through the castle with soldiers all around and be unseen. There was a maze of little passages leading to the main castle areas. One of these places was the great hall where Kings and Queens of Scotland had reigned. The hall was unoccupied and it did not look as if any kings or queens were living in the castle at that time. No children's playground could match this for the dreamers, as they were invisible and could do or imagine anything the wanted. They went out to the courtyard and visited the little chapel before making their way back to the parade ground and then out on to the Royal Mile, so called due to the castle being at one end and Holyrood Palace at the other.

Walking down from the castle the scenes that confronted them were anything but royal. The streets were filthy and the people were all poorly dressed and there were some lurking about to see who they could rob. From an alley a man was struggling out with a large canvas sack and as he loaded it on to a small cart the children could see that it contained a body. The man wheeled the cart away and the children saw that the man had a cloth tied round his nose and mouth.

Morag said, "I know what is causing this terrible time in Edinburgh. It is the time of the great plague and there was no cure for anyone catching the disease. It spread all over the city. I think this was in the year 1644."

As they walked along they could see the fear in the people's faces and it was not just from the plague for as they walked they could see dark passages or closes leading off and seeming to go down to other dark passages where people lived and there were also some business premises and small shops. With the plague these passages were not being cleaned and they were poorly lit. Continuing down the Royal Mile the children saw many bodies being taken away in carts and wheelbarrows.

There was also a large horse drawn cart loaded with bodies and the horse made the streets even more dirty. It looked as if the bodies were all being taken to be burned to keep the plague from spreading.

Torquil said, "I don't think that this visit to the past was to see Edinburgh Castle or to see the victims of the plague, although it may be part of the reason. I think we have still to find the main reason for our visit."

The four dreamers wandered down through the busier parts of the city, but there was no escaping the gloom and the fear on the people's faces. Walking back to the castle they decided to go down into one of the dark closes they had passed on the way down just to see the other side of the way of life in Edinburgh at that time in those confined little passages that sloped steeply down below street level. The ground was very uneven to walk on and as they left the area where daylight could penetrate to, there were oil lamps hanging on hooks fitted to the walls at each side of the small shops. There was very little light from the lamps and the oil used gave off foul smelling fumes as they burned.

As the dreamers wandered further down the passages people seemed to be lurking about in every dark recess and the children were glad nobody could see them. Well below ground now and the passages were darker with eerie looking chambers or cellars leading off on each side. This was now well past the area where there were any shops or small businesses and there were other passages leading off in different directions. Sounds were coming from a space and they crept forward to peer into an area on the right. The space in the wall opened out into a small cavern and the chanting was coming from there. The dreamers thought that it was people mourning someone who had died in the plague, but as that went closer the area was lit by candlelight and the chanting was coming from a group of women. They were all dressed in black cloaks and wearing pointed hats. They were standing round an object on the floor and as they chanted they were swinging weird looking trinkets on chains above the object on the floor. The object on the floor was a huge bowl with figures carved all around it. This was fascinating for the dreamers to watch, but they did not expect what happened next. From the large bowl a trickle of smoke drifted up and it became thicker and thicker until it almost reached the cavern roof. Then suddenly the smoke vanished and standing there in the centre of the women was a tall woman also in black with a pointed hat. She had her head bowed and when she raised it the four dreamers saw the most evil face they had ever seen in the flickering candlelight. She uttered some words and the women, or witches as they were now seen to be, started to dance around her, still chanting their weird song. The tall woman spoke again and the dancing and chanting stopped. One of the witches left the circle and went to the back of the cavern. She came back pulling a little lamb by a rope round its neck. She brought the lamb to the creature that had appeared from the smoke and it was lifted into the large bowl. It was now obvious that this was a witches' coven and they had used black magic to bring their leader from who knows where to offer her this sacrifice of the little lamb. The four dreamers had seen enough and rushed away along the narrow passage, but by this time they had lost all sense of direction and they were not sure which passage to take to get them out of there. There was a light from another small room and a big man was standing with his back to them. He wore a long black coat and was wearing a top hat. In the light of an oil lamp he had something in front of him on a long table. He struck downwards with a knife and there was a groan from the table. The children were off down the passage immediately. What was going to happen next?

The passage widened and they found themselves in a larger room and there were a lot of people walking about and talking to each other. The four dreamers breathed a sigh of relief to be along with ordinary people again after the horrible sights in the dark recesses and caverns of those grim closes. At least these people were more brightly dresses. Most had long white gowns and some looked ragged with long grey hair. Some were bald and they were all chatting and seeming very friendly. All were turning as if to leave this room and they had their backs to the children as they entered. The four dreamers just thought they would wend their way through these people and get back out on to the main street, but a man turned round to look in their direction. His face was pure white and the bones of his forehead and cheeks stood out. His mouth was open and a few teeth protruded from an open mouth. Morag felt so sorry for the man as he looked so ill and she thought that he must have the plague. Maybe all these people were suffering from it.

The Horror Of Old Edinburgh

Morag's sorrow was soon turned to absolute terror as the man lifted his arm and said,

"Welcome children, to the world of the dead." With that cry he shouted to the others and they all turned round. The four dreamers had never imagined that anything could look so ghastly as the faces of these people. They were walking skeletons. In fact they were all ghosts. They all waved to the children to come to them shouting in slow voices, “Come with us and live with the dead.”

They had hardly time to finish the word ‘dead’ before the dreamers had broken their clasped hands and were covered in mist. This return to Loch Brochan was the greatest moment of their lives. They were terrified by those ghosts and they had been so afraid that being in those deep passages the power of the loch would not be able to detect them and they would have been lost with the ghosts forever.

Calum said, “That is an experience that I never want to go through again. It will haunt me for the rest of my life. I never thought so much evil could be hiding in those dark closes of old Edinburgh.”

Morag said, “At first I felt sorry for those ghostly people and I still do because they will never know peace and will wander forever as ghosts. Only we, when we were ghosts from the future ourselves, can understand their grief.”

Torquil said, “What was the real purpose of the power of the loch taking us to see such evil and horror? Was it to show us that the way we live our lives will have an effect on us when we die? I think it was to make us understand that we must always do our very best every time we do anything, as we may not get a second chance.”

Flora said, “When we die will it be the same as it was when we were ghosts from the future visiting the past? If those apparitions we saw are ghosts their real bodies must be lying somewhere. They recognised us as ghosts also, but where were our bodies? Were they still lying on the shore of Loch Brochan when we were off on our trips to the past? What would happen if somebody found our bodies? They may have taken them away and we could not have been returned to them by the power of the loch. We could have been taken away to be buried.”

Flora’s speech brought silence from the four dreamers as they walked back to Strathbrochan. They all went straight home and from that day they never mentioned going back to Loch Brochan on an adventure as ghosts of the future to visit events of the past.

The four dreamers remained close friends and they always felt so privileged to have seen so many great things that had happened in the past and these will be for ever in their thoughts, but the last visit brought home to them that they must live an ordinary life and remember any lessons they learned on the trips to the past.

The villagers of Strathbrochan noticed that the four dreamers never went to Loch Brochan as often as they used to and they were missed by farmer Smith, but it was no use anyone asking why, because the dreamers had all agreed that the trips into the past were their special secret and they knew that no one would believe them anyway. This, however, did not stop their reputation as dreamers to be lost as they were always capable of spinning other tales to keep them in the news.

Strathbrochan gradually faded from the public eye and the village returned to normality and its leisurely pace of life once again.